Step

Step

Stories by
Deborah Ellis

Groundwood Books
House of Anansi Press
Toronto / Berkeley

Published in 2022 by Groundwood Books / House of Anansi Press
groundwoodbooks.com

Groundwood Books respectfully acknowledges that the land on which we operate
is the Traditional Territory of many Nations, including the Anishinabeg, the
Wendat and the Haudenosaunee. It is also the Treaty Lands of the Mississaugas
of the Credit.

We gratefully acknowledge for their financial support of our publishing program
the Canada Council for the Arts, the Ontario Arts Council and the Government
of Canada.

Canada Council   Conseil des Arts
for the Arts   du Canada

ONTARIO ARTS COUNCIL
CONSEIL DES ARTS DE L'ONTARIO
an Ontario government agency
un organisme du gouvernement de l'Ontario

With the participation of the Government of Canada   Canadä
Avec la participation du gouvernement du Canada

Library and Archives Canada Cataloguing in Publication
Title: Step / stories by Deborah Ellis.
Names: Ellis, Deborah, author.
Identifiers: Canadiana (print) 2021023329X | Canadiana (ebook) 20210233338
| ISBN 9781773065946 (hardcover) | ISBN 9781773068152 (softcover) |
ISBN 9781773065953 (EPUB)
Classification: LCC PS8559.L5494 S74 2022 | DDC jC813/.54—dc23

Jacket illustration by Clare Owen
Design by Michael Solomon
Printed and bound in Canada

Groundwood Books is a Global Certified Accessible™ (GCA by Benetech) publisher.
An ebook version of this book that meets stringent accessibility standards is available
to students and readers with print disabilities.

Groundwood Books is committed to protecting our natural environment. This book
is made of material from well-managed FSC®-certified forests, recycled materials and
other controlled sources.

MIX
Paper from
responsible sources
FSC   FSC® C016245
www.fsc.org

All royalties from the sale of this book will be donated to the United Nations High Commissioner for Refugees (UNHCR), which works to aid and protect people forced to flee their homes due to violence, conflict and persecution. www.unhcr.org

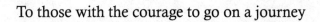

To those with the courage to go on a journey

Contents

1

Smash

Even on his eleventh birthday, Connor had to walk the dog.

It wasn't even his dog. It belonged to his sister. Janey had asked for a dog on her last birthday, when she turned thirteen. But not *this* dog. She wanted a little dog she could carry in her bag, like the celebrities did.

What she got was a mongrel from Mangy Mutts Rescue. It was the size of a beagle with the hair of a bad day.

"What am I supposed to do with this?" she whined.

"Take care of it," said Mom.

"Learn responsibility," said Dad.

Of course, she didn't. So of course, it fell to Connor.

"I didn't ask for a dog," Connor reminded his parents. "Make Janey do it."

His parents laughed at the idea of trying to make Janey do anything.

So, birthday or no birthday, Connor found himself once again, hat on head, jacket over jammies, dragging his sister's ugly mutt down the road to do his business. Instead of lying curled up warm in bed waiting for the scent of birthday apple pancakes to reach him, Connor was out in the world way too early with a creature who didn't want to be with him any more than he wanted to be with it.

The dog's name was Bentley.

"It's the name of a rich person's car," their mom had said, trying to get some kind of positive response out of Janey. Unlike Connor and Dad, Mom sometimes still had hope.

"I don't care what its name is!" Janey yelled before slamming the door. Or did she yell it after slamming?

So many yells. So much slamming.

Connor pulled Bentley to the end of their little street. He had to pull. Bentley was afraid of everything, even when, like now, they were the only ones awake on the planet. Bentley would have been happier to just do his business, then head back into the house to his spot in the corner of the kitchen, but Connor kept dragging him. He wanted Bentley to poop among the weeds of the wild area. That way he wouldn't have to pick it up and carry it home in a little bag.

He pulled Bentley across the road that went out to the country in one direction and toward the town in the other. Now they were in the undeveloped subdivision. Years ago, someone bulldozed the meadow, dug holes for basements and put in a paved road. Then they ran out of money.

The road still existed. Everything else was weeds.

While Bentley squatted, Connor thought again how much he hated that phrase. *Do your business.* Like the dog was a banker or something.

Connor sighed. He had thought that same thought yesterday, when he was ten. He'd hoped being eleven would bring him new thoughts. So far, same old.

Connor filled his lungs with cool fresh air and looked down the long stretch of road to nowhere. In the predawn light, the frost on the stubble and dead weeds made this abandoned area look like the set of a gangster movie. It was a perfect spot to dump a body.

The leash started to jiggle. Connor looked down. Bentley was on his back — away from his "business" — and wriggling, wriggling, wriggling in the frosty grass.

The dog had never done that before.

"Wow," said Connor. "Maybe there's more to you than being scared."

Bentley stopped wriggling and stared up at the blueing sky, belly to the air.

Slowly, slowly, Connor knelt down and ran his fingers in the soft hair of Bentley's chest. Bentley stretched his head back, exposing his throat, then curled his paws over Connor's hand, like he was praying.

They stayed like that for a long minute.

Then a bird chirped somewhere.

That was all it took to startle Bentley back to his feet.

Connor was about to take the dog home.

Then he had a thought.

He wasn't supposed to go any farther down the abandoned road than the patch of weeds Bentley used. He was not supposed to go exploring.

"We don't know what's down there," his mother said. It was the silliest reason ever not to explore someplace, but ten-year-old Connor had accepted it.

Eleven-year-old Connor was ready for something new.

He looked back at his street. He couldn't see his house from where he was, and no one was awake in there to see him anyway.

"Come on, Bentley. Let's go."

Usually, Bentley shook at the slightest sound and put the brakes on every two steps like he was being taken to his execution. But on this quiet morning, in this quiet place, with no cars or other people to frighten him, Bentley trotted beside Connor like a regular dog.

Feeling each one of his eleven years as he moved into unknown territory, with no adult to supervise and criticize, Connor walked with his head high.

He was not the first person to have traveled this road. He spied a rusty beer can and an empty rum bottle beside a flattened, faded firecracker box. He saw three car tires, six unmatched socks and a lawn flamingo without a head.

Connor could see that the road looped around in a big oval. In the middle of the oval were weeds, young trees and orange-painted sticks to show where the houses would go. One side of the oval backed onto a forest.

As Connor and Bentley rounded the bend, a deer stepped out of the weeds and onto the road. It stopped and looked at them calmly.

Dog and boy stayed absolutely still. Connor glanced down. Bentley was staring intently up at the deer, but he was not shaking.

The deer bobbed its head a couple of times, then strode casually into the woods.

Connor realized he had been holding his breath.

He exhaled, bent to scratch Bentley's ear, and they kept on walking.

There was no shortage of trash in the weeds. An umbrella skeleton, a lime green T-shirt covered in stains and snails, more beer cans and actual trash bags, ripped open with garden waste spilling out.

Up at the next bend, there was a mess of broken white pottery on the pavement.

Someone had smashed a plate.

Connor steered Bentley away from the mess, annoyed at the smasher who clearly gave no thought for the critters that might walk by here with tender feet.

Something on one of the pieces caught Connor's eye. It looked like hand-printed words. He picked it up and saw that the words were part of a sentence someone had written with a marker.

I'll never have any frien …

Connor picked up more pieces. All had words or parts of sentences on them.

I am ugl …

… aste my life …

… never be good enou …

No one knows the real…

Someone printed all these sad things on a plate. And then smashed the plate.

Why?

And who?

Connor gathered up the pieces with the most

writing, being careful to lead Bentley around the small pointy bits so he wouldn't get them in his paws. He put the pieces in his jacket pocket.

Then boy and dog headed for home. They went all around the rest of the oval, coming out where they had come in.

Back home, the downstairs was still quiet, but Connor heard sounds of waking up going on upstairs. He put food in Bentley's dish. Bentley was back in his corner of the kitchen, watching him and doing his usual shaking.

Which was the real Bentley? The scared dog in the corner? Or the roly-poly dog who went bravely with him into uncharted territory?

Connor looked at the clock. His parents were running late. No time for birthday apple pancakes.

Ten-year-old Connor might have held a grudge. But this older Connor? Who had been to a place no one else in his family had gone and had seen a deer while everyone else was still in bed?

This Connor washed his hands at the kitchen sink. He set the table and popped some frozen waffles into the toaster. He took the butter, syrup and orange juice out of the fridge.

When he closed the door, he saw the

family grocery list held up by a magnet they got at Niagara Falls.

Everyone in the family had printed an item they were running out of. Janey wanted almond milk and Fudgee-Os. Mom put down yogurt and paper towels. Dad had added peanut butter and oatmeal.

Each person's printing was a little bit different. Each person's printing also looked quite a lot like everyone else's.

Each person's printing looked like it could be the printing on the smashed plate.

Could someone in his family have written those sad things?

Connor watched them closely at breakfast. They all looked like they usually looked. His sister was carefully rumpled, an effect that had taken her an hour in front of the mirror to achieve. His mother was tidy and sharp in her gray suit. His father had on jeans and a plaid shirt since the dress code at his computer firm was more relaxed than at his mother's law firm.

His parents told him sorry and that the way he got breakfast ready showed he was growing up.

None of them seemed sad.

Which was the real family? The one in front of

him? Or was there a shadow family, with someone in it who was secretly sad and scared?

Connor chewed and watched, as if he could tell by looking at the members of his family who might have a secret sadness.

Halfway through his second waffle, Connor had a revelation. If everyone in his family had printing that looked sort of like the printing on the smashed plate, how many other people had printing that matched the smashed plate?

Anyone in the neighborhood could have written those things! Anyone in the town! Anyone in another town could have written them and then smashed that plate in a place where no one would see them.

Connor looked down at his own plate, smeared with syrup. What would it take for him to write sad things on it and then smash it? The smashing was just as important as the writing. Connor was sure of that. Maybe the smashing was a way of saying, "I'm done with all that!"

The sound of fingernailed paws on the linoleum made everyone in the family stop mid-chew.

The dog had left his corner.

The dog *never* left his corner.

No one moved. Forks full of waffles and mugs full of coffee hung suspended in the air, making the family look like they were in a magazine ad.

Bentley click-clicked his way to the table, stopped beside Connor's chair and plopped down on his belly with a "hmpppfff."

"Well," Dad said. "How about that?"

"I wonder what goes on in his head," Mom mused.

"Probably nothing," said Janey.

"We don't know what goes on in anybody's head," said Connor.

But he was going to try to find out.

And just like that, Connor took a giant leap forward, and decided to try to step into someone else's shoes.

2

Alone

Parents, teachers and everyone on the Disney Channel all say the same thing.

"You can be anything you want to be."

Well, what I wanted to be was alone.

On my eleventh birthday, I finally made it happen.

I began my escape with a lie to my teacher.

I got her attention in the schoolyard as she was trying to collect permission slips, check off names on a clipboard, hand out luggage tags and get twenty-eight kids and their stuff loaded onto a school bus.

"My uncle in Wyoming just died," I said, waving my phone at her like I'd just gotten a call. "I can't go on the class trip."

Ms. Blinsen blinked once, twice — like she was trying to remember if I was one of hers. After all, it was only the second week of school.

"Go tell the office," she said, then turned away to tell Carolyn Brown — again — to stop dangling gummy worms in Brandi Willard's face.

I zoomed into the school, straight to my locker. I grabbed my mother's old tent and the food I'd stashed away bundled up with my sleeping bag. I went to the bathroom one last time, then was back out on the playground in time to see the bus full of my classmates drive away.

As soon as the bus turned the corner, I left too, running two blocks over and three blocks up to the city bus stop. I got on the bus, paid my fare and took a seat, not quite believing I was actually doing what I had promised myself I would do.

Two bus changes, then I got off across the street from the east entrance to the Lipton County Nature Reserve. The main entrance was farther north. That's where the nature school was. My class was headed there for two nights of sleeping in cabins and outdoor education. They'd identify trees, learn about algae, study soil erosion and look for water spiders.

At least, that's what we did on the same trip last year, at the start of fifth grade. It was good stuff.

This year, I was going to do my own nature study.

The east entrance was a narrow gravel road, hardly ever used. I walked a short way in, then turned off the lane and found the path up the hill.

It was right where it used to be.

It was hard climbing up that hill loaded down with my pack and bedroll, but it felt good to be sweaty and achy.

At the top of the hill, I stopped and looked out at the view.

Down one side, I saw the campgrounds, with a few tents and trailers left over from the summer. I could get water there and use the outhouse. Down the other side was farmland, a gold and brown checkerboard going all the way to the edge of the world.

"I'm actually here," I said out loud. "I actually did it. Happy birthday to me!"

I couldn't stay in one of those regular campsites

because the park staff would come by to check that I'd paid and they'd start asking questions, and each lie I told them would just get me deeper into trouble.

So I couldn't stay there. But that was okay with me.

I had a better plan.

I hiked through the nature reserve until I came to the spot where Mom and I used to go for picnics.

"I found this place when I was a little girl," she told me once. "I was camping with my parents, packed myself a sandwich and spent the day exploring. I discovered *this*."

This was a circle of old willow trees, with branches gnarled and wavy, and long strings of leaves hanging like beaded curtains, slowly waltzing in the light breeze.

I walked into the middle of the circle and felt like I was home.

The light was shining down in beams through the leaves, the trees close enough to each other for the branches of one tree to grow and weave into another. The scent of the dried leaves on the ground, the sound they made when I shuffled through them, the feeling of being cut off from everyone in a secret world no one else knew about — it was all so familiar.

When I was a baby, I'd lie on a blanket and look up at those tree branches. When I was a toddler, I'd play with the sticks and sit on a low branch, held there by Mom's strong hands. When I was older, I'd climb the trees and try to go from tree to tree without touching the ground, but of course my arms and legs were too short to reach that far.

That was years ago.

I stood in the middle of the circle, put my stuff on the ground, looked up at the bits of sky showing through the many branches and laughed right out loud.

I emptied the tent bag and stared down at its contents.

The last time Mom took me camping, she set up the tent. I was little. I paid no attention to how she turned this pile of fabric and poles into a place for us to sleep. She was Mom. She made things work.

With no Mom and no instruction sheet, it took me forever to figure it out.

Finally I managed to put the poles together and

hook them into the tent rings. I got the tent up, then I tripped over a peg. The tent collapsed and I landed face down in the dirt.

I got myself up and kicked at the tent, which was pointless. I even thought about leaving the whole mess there and hiking to the nature school where I could be looked after by adults, but I got over that. I wiped the dirt from my face and clothes, set the tent up again, and felt like I had just built the Taj Mahal.

I crawled inside the tent and spread out my old Dora the Explorer sleeping bag, a Christmas present when I was six. I loved the musty smell of the tent and the way the sun and the trees planted shadows on the walls.

Next I opened my backpack and inventoried my supplies.

My food was stuff I'd saved from my packed school lunches and taken from the pantry in our kitchen. I had crackers and peanut butter, apples and pudding cups, granola bars and Fruit Roll-Ups.

I had a small bottle of hand sanitizer to use after I went to the outhouse. A flashlight with extra batteries. My Dora the Explorer binoculars — another

Christmas present from that same year — and three water bottles. I had an extra sweater and socks, and a ratty, practically memorized copy of *My Side of the Mountain*, a birthday gift from my parents when I was eight.

I zipped most of it inside the tent, picked up the water bottles and headed down to the camping area.

First stop was the outhouse.

I was scared of the outhouse. It would be dark and smelly and there would be spiders, although not poisonous ones. And even though I knew there would not be zombies waiting down below to bite my bottom, it still felt like there could be.

The nature school has real toilets, I thought. Then I told myself to smarten up. I would not trade my freedom for a toilet that flushed!

I put the water bottles on the ground and opened the door to the outhouse. Inside it *was* dark and smelly and there *were* spiders, but no zombies.

When I got out, swirling sanitizer on my hands, I felt like I had made it to the top of Mount Everest.

Then I walked to the campground's water tap.

I passed the campsite where Mom and I would

often camp, with Dad usually joining us for supper. It was empty now. A few campsites had tents, but not many. I had lies ready in case some grown-ups asked me what an eleven-year-old kid was doing wandering around by herself, but the few people I saw minded their own business and stayed out of mine.

I filled the water bottles and went back up the hill to my secret camp among the willows, and then I was done. No more chores.

I really wanted to have a campfire. I argued with myself about it for days before my escape. But I was breaking plenty of rules as it was. Lying to my teacher, lying to my parents, taking the bus by myself, camping in an unauthorized campsite. A campfire would be stretching my luck.

Maybe next time. If I did it right this time, there could be lots of next times.

I climbed onto a low, broad tree branch, leaned against the trunk and wondered what to do next.

I wasn't used to sitting still without a) a screen in front of me b) schoolwork or a book in front of me c) an adult-imposed sit-and-visit or d) an adult saying, "If you don't have anything to do, I'll find you something."

I made myself keep still. I listened to the quiet and discovered that the quiet was really full of sounds: rustling, chirping, croaking, buzzing. I heard chestnuts thud to the ground and squirrels chattering. A rabbit hopped by, sniffed at my tent, then hopped away.

No one knows where I am.

My whole self felt happy.

This *never* happens!

My parents gave me a cell phone, then put a tracker on it so they would know if I walked two steps away from where they've given me permission to walk. But the nature school is a No Phone Zone, so the tracking device is sitting in my locker. The school thinks I'm with my parents, and they can't check because Mom and Dad went off to some lodge where they can drink wine and be kid-free for a few days. I'll get home when they're expecting me, and no one will be the wiser.

I hope no one finds out that I'm not where I am supposed to be. I don't want anyone to worry. I wish there had been a way to do this without lying, but I couldn't think of one.

They want us to *play* Dora the Explorer. They

want us to *read My Side of the Mountain*. They just don't want us to actually go exploring and find our own mountain.

I eventually climbed down from the tree, ate some peanut butter right out of the jar followed by an apple. I spent most of the rest of the day at the pond. Actually, I was mostly *in* the pond, looking for turtles and squishing mud between my toes. I did not fall in and drown, not even once. Sometimes old-people campers walked by on the trail, but I ducked down in the bulrushes and they didn't see me.

Back at camp, my feet were caked with mud and smelling like swamp. I didn't want to get into my sleeping bag like that, and I didn't want to use up my supply of drinking water trying to get clean. So, I waited until dark and I hiked back down the hill by the east entrance, then followed the gravel road to the main road through the reserve, then followed that to the small swimming lake.

I had the beach all to myself. I waded in (the water was *cold*), washed the swamp off my legs, then sat down on the dock. I looked up at the stars and thought, This is what I want.

I headed back to camp. I had my flashlight with

me, but except for the trail, when I used it to make sure I didn't trip over anything, I didn't need it. My eyes got used to the dark. I could see fine.

My parents wouldn't even let me sit on our front porch by myself at night, let alone go for a walk by myself, not even just around the block.

Would they finally let me do that when I'm twelve? Fifteen? Twenty-five?

I got back to the circle of willow trees and, for a moment — okay, maybe longer — I was spooked. Everything looked different in the dark. The long, gently swaying branches that looked so friendly in the daylight now seemed evil. My imagination got going, and I stood outside the circle, getting eaten by mosquitoes, picturing all sorts of horrors lying in wait for me through the tentacles — wild dogs, bad men, giant snakes!

I had to make a choice. Either I stayed where I was and donated my blood to the mosquitoes, or I turned around and spent the night — where? On the dock? At the nature school?

Or I could brave up, walk right into that circle of willows and know that I would just deal with whatever was there.

I braved up.

There was nothing there. Just my tent, right where I'd left it.

Inside the tent, tucked into my sleeping bag, I ate a Fruit Roll-Up, then stretched out to sleep.

There was a rock under my back and a mosquito buzzing in my ear. I'd forgotten to bring a pillow, so I balled up a sweater and put it under my head. The ground was hard and cold, and I could not get comfortable.

At home, I fall asleep to the TV.

In the tent, with nothing to distract me, I was bugged by thoughts *and* mosquitoes.

Were Mom and Dad having a good time without me? Were they having a *better* time without me? When had I become such a drag to them? Was it when they got their important jobs? They used to do stuff with me. They used to think I was fun. At least, they acted like they did. But now it was all, "We're late for soccer." "You're the one who wanted to do judo." "How do you expect to get into college with grades like that?" "Did you practice your piano?" "If you're not going to pick up your clothes, we'll stop buying you nice things."

I'd turned into someone they had to nag and drive around.

I wouldn't want to spend time with me, either.

Between the rocks and the thoughts and the mosquitoes and no proper pillow, it was ages before I fell asleep.

But then I slept as solid as the rock underneath my back.

I woke up to a choir of birds and I felt pretty darn good.

I put my swimsuit on, put my clothes on over it and dashed down to the lake. There was still mist hovering over the glass-like water. I shucked my outer clothes, dashed into the lake and dove under the water, then I laughed because it was so cold and I was so happy.

I'd forgotten to pack a towel, so I put my clothes on over my wet suit and went back up to the willows. Breakfast was another apple and more peanut butter. This time I dipped pieces of granola bar into the peanut butter and it tasted really good.

I looked around at all the willow trees and wondered if I was finally big enough to do what I wanted to do when I was small. I decided to try it out.

Climbing up into one of the trees, I started working my way around the circle. Slowly, going from branch to branch, tree to tree, I made it all the way around.

Now, *that* was an accomplishment!

In the afternoon, I decided to check in with my class. I slung my binoculars around my neck and hiked to the hill overlooking the nature school. I sat down in the tall grass, hidden by trees and milkweed. I could see my class but they couldn't see me.

It was fun being a spy.

Jonathan and Jonah were trying to hit each other with their clipboards. Elsa, Arabela and Gail were peering into a square of grass, writing down all the forms of life they could see there. Arabela was being all serious, as usual, as if an accurate count of all the ants would guarantee her a place in a good university. Elsa was goofing off, pulling out blades of grass and tossing them onto Arabela's clipboard. Gail, also as usual, looked from one to the other, trying to decide who to side with.

There were kids by the stream studying erosion patterns. Others were measuring tree trunks. Ms. Blinsen was sitting with students at the picnic tables, making natural paints from berries and bark.

I heard screeching over at the stream. Glynnis and Kelda dashed away from the water. They probably saw a frog or, if they were lucky, a snake.

Who taught girls to squeal like that?

I've gone to school with most of these kids since kindergarten. I've been to some of their houses, and some of them have been to mine. There are kids I don't like and who don't like me, if they think about me at all. There are kids I avoid because, well, because everybody else does.

Sitting on that hill, I realized that I've spent a good chunk of my life with these kids, and I don't really know them at all. Then I thought, I've spent a good chunk of my life with my parents, too, and I really don't know them, either.

I took a closer look at my classmates. I saw Damon, one of the kids I avoided because everyone else did. He was off on his own, kneeling by the stream, building something with sticks and stones.

Had I ever talked to him outside of class? I didn't think so. Not that I could remember, anyway.

I scanned the whole area with the binoculars, looking at everyone.

Then I saw a glint of something in one of the trees.

I focused in on it.

Someone was looking back at me through their own binoculars!

I fell back in the grass and waited for the someone to give me away.

It didn't happen.

I looked again. As I was looking, the tree branches parted. A girl was sitting up there. Thelma, another of the Avoided. She waved at me, just a little. And just a little, I waved back.

Then I got out of there.

I didn't think she would rat me out, but if *she* spotted me, maybe someone else would, too.

I thought about Damon and Thelma as I walked back to my camp.

I moved my tent off the rock and onto a bed of dried leaves that might be a little softer to sleep on. I ate crackers and peanut butter and a pudding cup. I had to eat the pudding with a stick because I'd forgotten to pack a spoon, but the stick worked fine. I hiked back down to the lake to see the moon shine on the water. Then I went to bed and slept all night.

Now it's the morning of the last day, and I'm back in the tree. The birds are singing like it's a holiday.

Soon I'll have to take down the tent, pack everything up, and hike back out of here.

I don't want to go. I like my life here. But my parents will be home from their lodge this afternoon. I don't have much food left, and I'm not about to spend the winter in a hollow tree with a falcon to hunt for me, like Sam does in *My Side of the Mountain*. I did this escape to see if I could do it.

I did it.

I took the bus by myself — changed buses twice! — and I didn't get lost. I went for walks by myself after dark. I planned my own meals, put up a tent and used the dark, smelly, spider-infested-but-probably-not-zombie-infested outhouse so many times, it's like nothing now.

I need to find out what else I can do.

Maybe I can tell Mom and Dad that I'd like to go for a walk with them in the evenings. It would mean only a little time away from their work or their Netflix. Maybe if I help out more around the house — and pick up my clothes — they'll have more time to hang out with me. Maybe I can help them make dinner. Maybe I can make dinner for them.

Maybe they'll let me drop soccer and judo and take the bus to my piano lesson so they don't have to drive me around so much.

And maybe we can all come back to this nature reserve together and have a picnic here again, in the circle of willows.

But they won't know that's what I want unless I tell them.

It's time to go home.

When I need to, I know I can always step away.

And be alone.

3

Rock

Dom opened the small box from his brother. He stared at the smooth pink stone inside.

"It's a rose crystal," said Keith. "You hold it and it brings you good things. It's got magic powers."

"It does not," said Mom. "Unscientific nonsense."

"Crystals are a big business," Dad said. "A lot of people believe in them."

"A lot of people who need library cards," Mom snorted. She could snort like nobody's business.

"All I know is what the owner of the hippie store told me," Keith said quickly, before their parents took off in one of their disagreements. "She said if you hold a rose crystal it will give you confidence. You could take it to school …" Keith's voice trailed off.

"Look, Dom," said Mom, "the crystal is a pretty rock but that's all it is. You have everything you need inside you already. You have courage and confidence, intelligence, creativity and, most important, a kind heart."

Dom stared at the crystal and whispered thanks to his brother. Dad got up and started clearing the table. Mom picked up the remains of the birthday cake, and they headed to the kitchen.

"Looks like he's going to be the same at eleven as he was at ten," Dom heard Dad say before the door swung shut.

Dom and Keith were exempted from dishes when one of them had a birthday. Keith scraped the icing on his plate into a pile.

"It's going to get harder," Keith said. "Kids get meaner as they get older, and I'm not going to be able to help you next year."

In September, Keith was moving on to high school, leaving Dom alone at Willis Public. Kids picked on him there for not talking much, but they didn't pick on him too much. Keith was a big shot at the school, and everyone wanted to be on his good side.

With Keith gone, it was going to be open season on Dom.

Keith waited a few minutes in case Dom wanted to say something, then left the table. Dom gathered up his gifts and went to his room.

He put on his new birthday pajamas. The books from Dad — *David Copperfield* and a history of plagues — went onto his bookshelf. The binoculars from Mom — for bird watching and spy watching — went on top of his bureau by the window. The pizza socks from Auntie Heidy went into his sock drawer. The department store gift card from his grandfather went under his desk lamp.

Last was his brother's present. Dom tipped the rose crystal into his hand, then held it up to the light. White threads flowed through pink clouds.

"Unscientific nonsense," his mom had called it.

But what if she was wrong?

Dom closed his fist around the rock — tight, tighter, even tighter still. So tight his knuckles went white.

The bedroom started to shake, from the floor to

the drapes. Wind gusted in from somewhere. The room filled with swirling red dust, filling Dom's nose and eyes. He opened his mouth to call for help, and dust coated his tongue.

In the next moment, there was silence. The shaking stopped, the air grew still, and the dust fell like tiny red snowflakes, settling wherever it landed.

Every surface of his room was coated, from his bed to his bookshelf, from his bureau to the strange boy hunched in the corner.

Dom jumped to his feet. The strange boy looked just as startled. He jumped, too.

"Who are you?" they asked at the same time.

The stranger answered first.

"My name is Gregoire Rakotobe. I am from Anjoma Ramartina."

"Is that one of the new streets up behind the Canadian Tire?"

"It's in Madagascar."

"Madagascar? Where the lemurs are?"

"There are no lemurs where I live," Gregoire said. "What's your name?"

Dom told him. "What are you doing here?"

"You have my crystal."

Dom looked down at his hand that still clutched the pink stone. He loosened his fingers. The crystal was now caked with sweaty red dust.

"My brother gave it to me. Do you want it back?"

Gregoire laughed. "What would I do with it?"

"It's supposed to be magic," Dom answered. "It's supposed to bring you good things."

Gregoire laughed again, but without joy. "Our ground is full of these stones," he said. "If they are magic, why are we hungry?"

"Are you hungry?" Dom asked. Then, as he looked at Gregoire's thin arms and legs, he realized that was a silly question. "Wait here. I'll get you something."

Dom carefully opened his bedroom door, checked that the hallway was clear and dashed down to the kitchen.

In a flash, he was back with a plate of leftover chicken, potato salad and birthday cake. Gregoire ate it all. Dom noticed the boy was shivering, wearing just shorts and a torn T-shirt, even though the spring night was chilly. He gave Gregoire his bathrobe, and when Gregoire started to fall asleep in the chair, Dom led him to the bed and pulled up the covers. He got his sleeping bag out of the closet, unrolled it on the floor on top of the red dust, turned out the light and crawled in.

Just as he was drifting off, he heard Gregoire say, "You can keep the stone. I just want two things. I want a full bag of rice. And I want a new dress for my mother. Not too fancy. If it's too fancy, she won't wear it. But I want her to feel beautiful when she goes to church."

A bag of rice and a new dress. Dom thought of the department store gift card from his grandfather. He wondered how much a dress cost.

I'm having a sleepover, he realized. He was so surprised, he didn't even think about all the talking he had just done.

The next day was Saturday. Dom woke up early, fetched them both bowls of ccreal, showed Gregoire how to use the shower so he could wash off the red dust and gave him warm clothes and shoes from his closet. They were out the door before anyone else was awake.

The department store was on the edge of town, just over a mile from Dom's house. He walked there next to Gregoire, walking and talking the way he'd seen other kids do. He watched himself as if from a distance, acting like a regular kid with an actual friend.

Then he got caught up in the conversation, forgot about himself, and just was.

Gregoire had many questions about Dom and Dom's world, and Dom had many questions about Gregoire and his world. Dom learned about the village in Anjoma Ramartina where Gregoire lived with his parents and five younger brothers and sisters. He learned about the dusty red earth that was littered with sharp-edged crystals that cut their feet when they could not afford shoes, about the soft ground that caved in on them when they were digging out the stones, and about which of the roadside stands sold the best spicy spinach fritters. Dom learned about Gregoire's baby brother, Angel, who died when bandits stole the crystals they'd dug up and there was no money for food.

"That's why I want a whole bag of rice," Gregoire said. "We can dig crystals all day and only get just enough money for one cup of rice. I want a whole bag of rice so that we will always have food."

Dom learned that Gregoire had not been to school in a long time. "But when I am there, I am

Chief of Arithmetic! Go ahead. Test me!"

They had time for five multiplication problems before arriving at the department store.

Gregoire's jaw dropped. "All these things! Look at all the toys! Look at all the food!"

They walked through the store, Gregoire exclaiming over everything, but Dom saw the things on the shelves with new eyes.

There was so much stuff! Dog toys that looked like monkeys. Shelves full of garbage cans. Small boxes to store things in and bigger boxes to hold the small boxes. Stuff to add to coffee to make it not taste like coffee.

Dom found it all a bit embarrassing.

They arrived at the dress section. Gregoire looked at each dress carefully, as if he was trying to imagine his mom wearing it. He settled on a light blue dress with a white collar.

"It's the color of the sky," he said.

Dom checked the price tag. There was just enough money on his gift card to cover the cost of the dress plus the taxes.

He led Gregoire up to the cashier and then froze. He had never paid for anything himself before. His parents were always trying to get him to do it, but he always refused, and they didn't press it.

Dom was afraid the cashier would say something to him. Then he would have to say something back. The whole idea of it was overwhelming.

But today there was no choice. Gregoire had never been in a store like this. Dom had to do it.

The cashier was a giant of a man with a big beard and a scowl. He looked down at Dom from a hundred feet up.

Trembling, Dom held out his gift card, feeling like Oliver Twist holding out his gruel bowl, about to ask for more.

Scowly Beard took the card and processed the sale.

"Nice dress," he said. "My mom has one just like it."

He put the dress in a bag, then handed Dom back the gift card. "You've got seventy-six cents left. Have a nice day."

And that was that.

They left the store.

They were a block away when Dom realized something. "We forgot to get rice!"

"That's okay," said Gregoire. "The dress is the important thing."

"No, no, we'll get rice, too. I'll have to get some

more money. Maybe my brother will lend it to me. He's a pretty good brother. Everyone likes him — teachers, neighbors, other kids. He gets along with everybody. I don't get along with anybody. It's never enough with other people. You say one thing and they expect you to keep saying things, and when you run out of things to say, you can't just say, 'I have no more to say,' and be done with it. They just won't leave you alone. Do you know what I mean?"

When Gregoire didn't answer, Dom turned to look at him.

Gregoire was not there.

Ten feet behind Dom, there was a pile of clothes on the sidewalk — the jacket, trackpants and shoes Dom had given to Gregoire. The bag with the dress was there, too.

Gregoire was gone.

Dom stood alone on the sidewalk, feeling more alone than he ever had before.

Finally, he picked up the clothes and the bag and walked home by himself.

A mile gave him a lot of time to think. By the time he got home, Dom knew what he was going to do.

His family were all in the kitchen, so he was able to go into the house without them seeing him. He went straight to his room and straight onto his computer.

He looked up the name of the village Gregoire came from and found a news story about how a crystal mine had collapsed. Several people had been injured. One had died.

The name of the dead boy was Gregoire Rakotobe.

Dom kept researching. An article about Gregoire's family mentioned the church they attended, and Dom found the address of that church. He learned about the thousands of children working in Madagascar's crystal mines. He learned that most of them lived in homes without electricity or running water, and that most did not go to school or get enough to eat. He learned that the mine owners got rich off their labor.

Dom read until his brain was full.

Then he went downstairs.

And stepped into the kitchen to talk to his family.

He talked and talked. He told them about Gregoire and the mines and the dress he had bought. He talked and they sat and listened and did not interrupt him until he had run out of words.

When he was done, his dad leaned forward, took hold of his hand and asked, "How can we help?"

Monday morning before school, Mom drove Dom to the post office and stood behind him while he mailed the dress to Gregoire's mother, care of her church, along with a note that said, *In memory of your son.* He also sent a money order, with contributions from Mom, Dad and Keith — enough to buy several full bags of rice. Mom dropped him off at school, telling him how proud she was of him. It was nice to hear, but Dom knew he hadn't done enough.

He went to the library at lunch time. He had never spoken to the librarian before. Why talk when he could read? But today he needed her help. He stepped up to her desk and asked. She was so surprised she almost spit out her coffee. But she recovered, and together they got to work.

After school, Dom went to the hippie store. He'd been there before with his mom, during her scented-candle phase. He went inside, inhaled a cloud of incense and stepped right over to the crystal display.

A man and woman were looking at the stones. Leaning against the wall, as far from the adults as possible, was a boy about Dom's age, looking bored out of his skull.

Dom stepped up to the customers.

"You should know that a lot of crystals are mined by children living in poverty," he said in a clear voice. "Sometimes they get hurt. The dust from the stones can give them cancer. Sometimes they die. Here is a leaflet I made to tell you about it." He held out the leaflet the school librarian had helped him make.

"What's going on?" The owner of the shop hurried over to them.

"I'd like to tell you about the children who dug up your crystals —"

"I'm spiritually attracted to this blue stone," one of the customers interrupted. "Can you tell me about its powers?"

"You don't need crystals to make you feel better," Dom told them. "You have everything you need inside of you already!"

"I'll be right with you," the owner said, before

escorting Dom out of the store and onto the side-walk. "This is my place of business, young man! Stay out. Unless you want to buy something," she added. She returned to her customers.

Dom was shaking inside and out, but he also felt good. He handed a leaflet to a woman walking by with her young daughter. His voice warbled a bit as he spoke to them, but he got the words out.

"Cool speech," he heard someone say. He looked and saw it was the boy from the hippie store. "I've tried to tell them but they don't want to hear it." He wiggled his fingers at the flyers. Dom handed him some. "They will freak when they come out and see me doing this," the boy said happily. "What's your name?"

"Dom. What's yours?"

"Greg."

Dom smiled.

He kept stepping forward.

4

Rubber

Oma has been eleven years old for seventeen minutes.

There is just enough moonlight in the cove for her to see the small fleet of rubber rafts and the big crowd of people waiting to get on them.

"It's just a short boat ride," Father says. "Rich people on holiday cruise this sea all the time."

Oma has seen the pictures. For rich people, the sea is glass-green and the sky is a clear, bright blue.

For her family, the sea is a dark, crashing monster, ready to swallow them up.

"They probably pay less for their trip than what

this one is costing us," says Mother. Then, remembering her promise to stay positive, she adds, "We will have a wonderful view of the stars once we're out on the water."

"Do you think we'll see a falling star?" asks Coman, Oma's nine-year-old brother.

When her parents don't answer, Oma looks up and sees the crease in her father's forehead and the tightening of her mother's lips.

"I'll see one before you do," she says, answering for them.

The four of them stand on the ridge a moment, listening to the sounds of the water and the people.

"We're not going to get to Europe by standing around in scratchy beach grass," Mother says.

She grabs hold of Oma's hand. Oma is far too old to hold her mother's hand, but she doesn't pull away. With Father holding on to Coman and Mother holding on to Father and Oma, they make their way down the ridge and onto the beach.

On the sand, smugglers wave flashlight beams like searchlights, making the darkness darker and momentarily blinding Oma in swift brightness. She stumbles over a rock. Mother's strong arm keeps her from falling.

They go from flashlight carrier to flashlight carrier, looking for the smuggler who has their names on his list.

They finally find him standing in front of two rubber boats pulled up on the sand.

"Family of four," the man says, popping a piece of gum in his mouth. Oma smells a hint of peppermint, then the wind from the sea takes it away. The smuggler stares at Oma and her brother. "You said they were small."

"They are," says Father.

"They're nearly grown. They'll take up more room. That will cost you more money."

Oma feels her mother's grip on her hand tighten.

"We have already given you a great deal of money," Dad says.

"More money now or one of the children stays behind," the smuggler says. "Or take both children and leave your wife. Or you stay back. You think it matters to me? Decide now."

The smuggler holds out his hand. Father takes off his wristwatch. It is a good watch, a present from his grandfather for graduating university. Oma knows the family was hoping to sell it in Europe to pay for food.

The smuggler shines the flashlight on the watch, then pushes it onto his own wrist.

"Better with me than at the bottom of the sea, eh?" His laugh sounds like a dog snorting. He tosses them four life jackets. "Stay in this spot. We're loading soon."

"Soon" does not feel like soon to Oma. She and Coman stand as close as they can to each other and to their parents. They listen to the smuggler take more payment from all the other families who are booked onto his boats.

"Ajmal! Ajmal!"

A man runs up to Oma's father with his family in tow.

"Fadil!"

Oma recognizes the family. They used to live two streets over in their old neighborhood. There are hugs all around. Back home, Oma never really liked this family. Their things were always slightly better than her family's things. Their kids were always slightly better dressed, and Oma thought that made them a bit stuck-up.

But here, in this strange place, she is very glad to see them.

"You are on these two boats?" Fadil asks Oma's

father.

"Yes. Well, one of them."

"You should split the family up," Fadil says. "That's what we are doing. Some in one boat, some in another. That way, if the sea is rough — well, better chance at least some of us will make it."

"I don't know …" says Oma's father.

"Trust me, it's the best way. Oh, our boats are boarding. See you on the other side!"

"As God wills it," Oma's father calls after them.

Oma's father and mother look at each other. Oma is afraid they will make a decision she doesn't like, so she pipes up.

"All of us together!"

Her brother nods fiercely.

Her parents nod more slowly.

"All of us together," they agree.

Father takes two handfuls of strong cord out of his pocket and hands one to Oma's mother. They practiced this, so Oma knows what to expect as Mother ties one end of the cord around Oma's wrist and the other end around her own. Father does the same with Oma's brother.

"If the cord breaks once we land, stay where

you are," Father reminds them. "We will come to you. There might be a crush of people and we don't want to lose you."

The smuggler calls out, "Get on the boats!"

People rush to pile on. The round, smooth wet sides of the inflatable dinghy are difficult to climb over. Oma helps her mother and they both fall back against other passengers. They right themselves up, apologize to those they slammed into, and are slammed into themselves by even more people piling on.

Someone bops Oma in the head. She turns around to see her brother making one of his ugly faces at her. Father is beside him. She makes an ugly face back at her brother, then grins at them both. She is glad they are close.

The dinghy is pushed out to sea.

The waves are big. It only takes three of them for the woman next to Oma to throw up.

Oma is packed in so tight she can't even move her arms to wipe the vomit from her knees.

She has been eleven years old for two hours and thirty-five minutes.

• • •

"Are we there yet?"

Oma hears her brother's question. She knows he is asking their father, but some stranger answers.

"If we were there, would we still be in this boat?"

"I just wondered if we were getting close."

"I've got enough to worry about without having to listen to children whining," says the stranger. "Keep him quiet or he'll be the first one overboard."

"Keep quiet yourself," Oma hears an old woman call out to him. "You're not the mayor of anything anymore!"

"I am still the mayor of —"

"Your town has been bombed into garbage," says the old woman. "You want to be mayor of garbage town? Go ahead. Go on back. But on this boat, you're just another person. Leave the boy alone."

"All of you shut up!" the smuggler yelled. "You didn't pay me enough to have to listen to you."

Oma's father touches her shoulder, and she leans back to listen to him say quietly to her and her brother, "I think we should reach Europe by morning. The crossing is only supposed to take a few hours."

Oma looks to her right. They are heading north, so right is where the east should be. The sky is a little lighter over there, she thinks. Maybe.

It is already morning somewhere.

Oma has been eleven years old for four hours and fifty-six minutes.

"Someone's coming!"

Oma sees a bright light from the west getting closer and closer.

"We're getting turned back!"

"No, we're being rescued!"

The population of the boat is divided about what is going on. With so many people bigger than her, Oma has a hard time seeing anything.

Then she does.

A real boat — not one made of rubber — pulls up alongside theirs. It is twice as long as their dinghy and three times as high, with a cabin on top. The men on the bigger boat turn on spotlights, making everyone in the dinghy wriggle to free their arms to shield their eyes.

"Get out your jewelry," one of the men orders over

a loudspeaker. "We want it all. Rings. Necklaces. Bracelets. Passports, too, and wallets. Get it all out."

Men hop from the larger boat onto Oma's, making the dinghy rock from side to side. There is screaming. Oma hears slapping. She sees the smuggler helping the thieves, then taking the motor off the dinghy and lifting it onto the larger boat.

The thieves push and shove as they steal from everybody. They yank Mother's thin gold chain right off her neck. It had been her mother's, and her grandmother's before that. They grab Oma's hair to look for earrings. She screams and tries to pull away. The man hits her in the head and moves on to someone else.

With everyone robbed, the thieves and the smuggler leave the dinghy and sail away into the pistol-gray dawn.

Oma has been eleven years old for six hours and nineteen minutes.

Dawn brings fear, not relief, as the land that Oma expects to see is nowhere in sight. The sea is flat now, and the sky has turned from gray to the bright blue of the rich people's cruise pictures. The brighter the blue, the bigger Oma's thirst.

Oma's legs cramp from being squished in one position for so long. She tries to move them around. The woman next to her pushes against her.

"This is my space," the woman says.

"We're all in the same boat," Mother tells her.

Behind them, Coman laughs. He and Oma have heard their mother say that a million times — when the power went out, when the taps ran dry, when the sandstorms blasted and when bombs fell.

"This time we really are in the same boat!" Coman says. It's the sort of humor he likes. He smacks Oma between her shoulder blades to make sure she appreciates his wit.

Oma shows great maturity and does not smack him back. She tells him his joke is funny, even though it isn't.

The dinghy floats without traveling. A few young people start to sing. Some old people tell them to knock it off, no one wants to hear it. The young people remind the old ones that music is a gift from God, and if they don't want to hear it, they are welcome to go somewhere else.

The young people sing a song Oma knows, a song about freedom and standing together.

"You can get thrown in jail for singing songs like that!" Oma hears the former mayor yell at them.

"That's why we are all in this boat," Mother says. "Because we are tired of living under governments that are afraid of songs."

The former mayor shuts up. The singing starts again. Mother whispers to her neighbor, and the neighbor passes Mother's message along. After a few more passes, the message reaches the singers.

They sing "Happy Birthday" to Oma.

She has been eleven years old for ten hours and fifteen minutes.

As the day goes on, Oma's throat gets dryer, her stomach gets emptier and her bladder gets fuller. She looks and looks for land. She doesn't see any.

She turns to her mother to tell her that she has to go to the bathroom, but her mother is sleeping.

Oma doesn't wake her.

She is eleven now. She should be old enough to figure things like this out for herself. But she doesn't know how. She does not want to wet herself and look like a baby in front of her little brother, but from the smells around her, she guesses that this is how others on the boat have addressed this problem.

"Dress in layers," Father said before they left. "I heard they won't let people take luggage on board, so wear everything you'll need for the trip."

That was fine in the cold dark night, but the sun is now making Oma feel like a too-big bread roll being baked in a too-small oven with too many other bread rolls.

Oma is completely consumed by two opposite urgencies — the need to take in water and the need to get rid of water.

She has been eleven years old for thirteen hours and twenty-two minutes.

"A ship! It's a ship!"

Oma is jolted into alertness. The dinghy unsettles in the water as people turn and try to stand to get a glimpse. The wind has come up. The boat does not need any more rocking.

"We're going to be rescued!"

"We're going to be attacked again!"

"Use your arms! Paddle toward them!"

"No! Paddle away!"

The rocking gets worse. Oma hears a cry as the

boat tips and someone slides out and into the water. Arms stretch out to grab the person, but the sea takes the dinghy in one direction and the overboard person in another. Oma thinks she sees a spot of orange life vest, but just for an instant. Then the waves take over and she doesn't see it again.

Now there is crying as well as screaming, and more boat rocking and more arguments between the "Settle down!" and the "Do something!" folks. Oma finds herself being jealous of the people who were in the row the overboard person fell out of. They have more room to move now. She hates herself for having these feelings.

"It's getting closer!"

Now there is panic in the dinghy that the bigger boat won't see them, that it will plow right into them and send them all tumbling into the sea.

Oma feels her father's hand on her shoulder.

"Keep calm," he says. "We think better when we're calm."

"We'll be all right," Coman says in the voice he used to try to convince everyone he was brave when their town was bombed. "I'm the swimming champion in my grade. I'll save us if we go in the water."

"No one is going in the water," says Mother in the same voice she uses to say that no one is going to eat the cake reserved for company. She checks the cord around Oma's wrist and then her own, tells Father to do the same with Coman, then sits up straight, ready for what comes next.

This boat is a yacht, bigger than the boat belonging to the thieves. It rides high out of the water, but not so high that Oma can't make out the people on the deck. They are holding drinks and wearing bright colors. The yacht comes very close to the dinghy but does not hit it. The waves made by the moving boat add to the waves made by the wind, and three more people slide into the water.

By making a human chain, the people in Oma's dinghy are able to pull one of the people back on board, but the ship turns back around again. Two more people disappear in the waves.

"Help us!" the dinghy people call out to the people on the yacht. They call it out in English and Arabic, French and German and Italian — in all the languages the dinghy people know.

"Go back to where you came from!" yells out one of the yacht people. They sail away, leaving the dinghy bobbing like a cork in the wide cruel sea. Going nowhere.

Oma has been eleven years old for fifteen hours and thirty-two minutes.

Oma wakes up to a dark, cloudy sky. She realizes that she wet herself while she was asleep. She feels humiliated, certain that everyone knows.

The waves are much higher. The wind seems to be blowing in many directions at the same time.

A huge wave hits the dinghy — so huge it drenches even Oma and her family sitting in the middle of the boat.

"We're sinking!"

"Get the water out!"

Oma sees people trying to bail with their hands, tossing the sea out of the boat one handful at a time.

Another wave hits, and another. Sea water soaks through the many layers of Oma's clothing.

The sea gets rougher, the sky gets darker, and Oma has been eleven years old for one million years.

Oma is belly down in wet sand. Pain is in every

part of her body. Her head is full of fog and her throat is full of grit.

Something pulls on her wrist. She thinks it is a thief, come to steal her arm. She thinks it is one of the overboard people, pulling on her to save them.

She tries to pull away.

"Oma, Oma! It's all right!"

Her mother's voice reaches her through the fog. Slowly, painfully, she turns her head.

Mother is beside her on the sand. Beyond her, Oma can see other people. Some are on the sand. Some are dragging themselves out of the water. She sees her brother and father among them.

She raises herself up. Her left ankle buckles under her, so she leans against her mother.

She takes a step into this new world.

She is eleven years old.

5

Shoes

_____

Lazlo's just-turned-eleven-year-old legs can almost keep up with his father's.

"Where are we going?" he asks. "I'll bet we're going to the catacombs. All year, you've been saying, 'Maybe on your birthday.' Are we going to the catacombs?"

"Ask me again, I'll dump you in the Danube," says his father.

Lazlo laughs. He stretches out his legs so that, for a brief instant, his stride perfectly matches his father's. It's not something he can keep up for long, but he's happy to be able to do it at all.

They enter Kossuth Square, by the monumental Hungarian parliament buildings, majestic and beautiful. Lazlo's chest swells with pride. Budapest is a grand city, and it makes him feel grand just to be a part of it.

Lazlo likes history, especially Hungarian history, because it is his history. Many of his classmates think history is just boring ramblings in a book, but to Lazlo, history is alive. It's all around him every day.

He can see it in the old buildings and the cobblestone streets, in the bridges and the way the River Danube divides Buda and Pest. He can taste history in goulash, Hungary's national dish that can be traced back one thousand years. He can hear it in the traditional music they sing in the school choir.

Sometimes, if he's in the right spot and in the right mood, he can feel the ghosts of Hungarians past, walking where he walks, seeing and hearing and feeling what he sees and hears and feels.

He wants to ask again where they're going, but he doesn't. It's a surprise outing, just for him and his father, so he knows it's going to be great.

Lazlo tells himself that anywhere will do, but he is really hoping for the labyrinth under Buda Castle, the warren of tunnels that was once used as a prison and torture chamber. Vlad Tepes — Vlad the Impaler, the original Dracula — was one of the prisoners kept there. And it has a new sound and light show with fog and everything!

Lazlo feels a bit guilty, being fascinated by a place where people did such horrible things to each other. Maybe Vlad the Impaler had it coming to him, but most of the others held in that place probably didn't. They were enemies of the ruler or in the wrong place at the wrong time.

But all of that happened long ago, and Lazlo didn't know any of those people. Maybe that makes it all right to be fascinated.

He wishes he could talk to someone about this. If there is one thing that studying history has taught him, it's that human beings have always been the same, with the same bunch of feelings they have today — feeling mad, amazed, jealous, sad, happy. If something is bothering Lazlo now, someone else will have been bothered by the same thing. And maybe they would know how to deal with it.

He can't talk to his brother or sister. Josef, two years older, spends all his time drawing complicated Japanese anime. His sister, Maria, three years older, wants to be something on Instagram, although Lazlo has a hard time figuring out what.

"My one Hungarian child," his father calls him, and that makes him feel pretty good.

So wherever they're going — up the funicular to Buda Castle and the Old Town, or to the market filled with food, food and more food, or the thermal baths or wherever — it will be a great birthday excursion. Afterwards, they'll go home where his mother is preparing a birthday feast with hunter stew and a birthday cake so beautifully decorated with hand-drawn flowers, Lazlo couldn't believe it was to be his.

"Maybe this year I could have some peach brandy?" he asks his father.

"You think you're man enough?"

"Absolutely."

"We'll see."

Lazlo watched both his sister and brother try the

traditional birthday drink. Both pushed it aside after one sip and chose Coke instead.

He, Lazlo, would not do that!

They reach the banks of the Danube, and Lazlo sees the chain bridge not too far away.

He knew it! They'll cross the bridge, ride the funicular up to the castle (or maybe walk up, since they're men, after all!) and go to the labyrinth. Or maybe his dad is taking him on a boat ride down the Danube.

Lazlo wants to jump up and down like a little kid, but he restrains himself. He is eleven now, old enough to play it cool.

His father leads him across the road to the pathway along the river. He doesn't make way for anybody — not joggers, not cyclists, not old men with canes or women pushing strollers, and certainly not for teenagers bent over their cell phones.

Lazlo's chest gets bigger every time he sees the oncomers swerve or step aside for them. When a phone-staring teenager protests as they knock into him, his father doesn't even respond.

We go where we want and we do what we want, Lazlo thinks.

A few dozen men are standing in the promenade

ahead of them. There is one narrow pathway everyone must go through to get past them. Like Lazlo's father, the men don't step aside for anybody. They are big and tough-looking, with lots of leather vests and strong arms bursting out of short sleeves.

Lazlo ducks behind his father who will not be afraid to move right through this group. And he, Lazlo, will follow in his father's footsteps.

"Lakszi!"

Lazlo hears a man call out his father's name and sees several of the group raise their hands in greeting.

"You're late."

"Boy slowed me down," Dad says.

"Boy? What boy? You mean that rabbit behind you?"

Lazlo's face burns with shame as his father reaches back and pulls him forward.

"Maybe he's a rabbit, maybe he's a wolf," says his dad. "Remains to be seen. I have hopes for this one. The other two are a washout."

His dad has hopes for him! Lazlo smiles and stands a little taller.

"Let's take a look at him," the man says. He

takes a step toward Lazlo and holds out his hand. "I'm Oden. Old friend of your father's."

Lazlo shakes Oden's hand, deliberately not letting his face wince at the man's grip.

"You might have a winner here," Oden says to his father. "Square up those shoulders, boy."

Lazlo does.

"That's it. Always stand proud. How old are you? Fourteen?"

"Eleven," says Lazlo. "Today."

The men crowd around to shake his hand and wish him happy birthday. They speculate on the number of girlfriends he must have.

"What are you doing to celebrate?"

"We're maybe going to the catacombs," Lazlo says hopefully, looking to his father for confirmation.

"You don't want to go there," says Oden. "Full of foreigners. Tourists. You want to spend your birthday with your fellow Hungarians."

"It's time," someone says.

"Keep your skirt on," Oden says, and everyone laughs, including Lazlo, although he's not sure what's funny. "All right. Let's begin."

The men spread out a little and open up Lazlo's

view. He sees the mighty Danube sparkling in the sunlight, boats going by, and the ancient castle on the hill.

He also sees a line of black iron shoes on the river's edge, toes pointing to the water.

The shoes are old-fashioned, from the 1940s. There are women's shoes with heels, men's working boots and children's shoes. There are shoes for everyone, looking like their owners have just stepped out of them. Many of the shoes have flowers sticking out of where the feet would go.

Lazlo stares at the shoes. He knows what he is looking at. He has learned about this place in school, although he has never been here before.

"Hail Hungary!" Oden yells suddenly, making Lazlo jump in his skin.

"Hail Hungary!" the men shout back, over and over, like they are cheering at a football match.

Oden takes something out of his pocket, gives it a shake and pulls it onto his arm.

It is an armband with the Nazi symbol on it. Lazlo learned about that in school, too.

Lazlo wants to leave. He turns to his father to ask if they can go, and his eyes grow wide at the sight of his father pulling on a Nazi armband, too. His father winks at him, slaps the arm band like he is brag-slapping a muscle, then takes another armband out of his pocket and hands it to Lazlo.

Lazlo takes it, too shocked to know what else to do.

"Some artist made these shoes to be a memorial to the Jews who were shot here by the Arrow Cross over seventy-five years ago," Oden proclaims. "It is billed as a sad place. People leave flowers like they do on a grave. But we are here today to celebrate a time when Hungary was strong, when Hungary was brave! And we are here to say, it is time for us to be strong again! My brothers, advance and unfurl your banners!"

Four men move to stand beside Oden and they unroll two banners. One reads, Hungary for Hungarians! The other says, Kick Out Migrants!

There is more shouting, and arms are raised in the salute Lazlo has seen in the history books and on film.

He is shoved on his shoulder. His father is glaring at him, wanting him to raise his arm.

"I see we have a hesitater," Oden says, looking

right at Lazlo. "We have a young man here whose head has been filled with lies. He is confused. Step forward, birthday boy. Time to be a man with a clear head and a strong heart."

Lazlo is pushed from behind by more arms than just his father's.

Oden turns Lazlo around to face the crowd. "I give you the future of Hungary. Hail Hungary! Hail Hungary!"

Lazlo can't bear to look at his father, and then he does. He sees pride in his father's eyes and an encouraging smile on his father's face. All the men are smiling. All are encouraging. He is being welcomed as a man among men, and from this day forward, he could always be golden in his father's eyes.

"Pick up that flower," Oden says to Lazlo.

He is pointing at a red rose sticking up out of a child's iron boot.

Lazlo picks it up, careful of the thorns.

"Very good," says Oden. "Now, drop it in the water. Show the world that this is not a place of mourning, but a place of beginning. Show the world that you are a leader in the building up of a new Hungary!"

Lazlo turns and faces the river.

It's just a flower, he thinks. It means nothing. It will die soon anyway, out here in the sun.

He can't help but see the long row of iron shoes bolted to the concrete, facing the river. He remembers from school that people had to take their shoes off before they were shot because the shoes were valuable. The killers did not want the shoes going into the river still attached to the people they were killing.

How did those people feel as they removed their shoes and stood on the riverbank? Did they hope they would not be shot? Did they hope the soldiers were just playing with them, just torturing them, as they had seen happen to so many, over and over and over and over?

"It takes courage to go against what you've been taught," Oden says to him. "That is why you are hesitating. Drop the flower. Let the Danube carry it away. And with it, may it carry away all your fears and hesitations, so that what you have left is pure strength."

Lazlo looks down at the water.

This is what they saw, he thinks. They looked at the river and they didn't want to die. It was their river, they were Hungarians, and it was going to carry them away, and the men who were going to shoot them would never think about them again.

He could fit into some of the shoes. He knows by looking at them that they would fit him. Some of the bodies that hit the river with bullets in their heads had been his age, even younger.

Maybe for some of them, it was even their birthday.

He clutches the red rose so tightly he can feel the thorn go into his hand.

Lazlo turns and looks at his father. He has one question.

"Does Mama know?"

But Lazlo does not want to hear the answer. If his mother knows, there is a problem. If she does not know, there is another problem.

Lazlo stretches out his hand and drops the Nazi armband into the Danube.

Then he steps away from his father. And keeps stepping.

He keeps on stepping until he is on the chain bridge and then across it.

From the other side of the river, the big men look very small.

Lazlo does not go up the funicular. He does not take himself to the catacombs beneath Buda Castle. He has had enough horror.

It's flowers he wants, lots and lots of living flowers. He will find a garden, a big one, and place into it the rose that he is still carrying.

Then he will sit down beside it, and try to figure out what the hell to do next.

6

Ride

This year, Aislyn's eleventh birthday fell on the opening day of the county fair. To make the day even better, instead of going with her parents, her older sister, Laura, was going to take her.

"We'll be fine," Laura insisted when their parents looked at each other and frowned. "We won't leave the fairgrounds, we won't get into trouble and we won't take candy from strangers." She counts them off on her fingers in a bored voice. "Besides, since I started high school, Aislyn and I hardly get to spend any time together."

Aislyn could have said that Laura had not wanted to spend time with her for years, and that entering ninth grade had nothing to do with that, but why would she? An evening with her sister at the fair would be a thousand times better than going with her parents.

Their parents finally gave in, as Aislyn knew they would. They didn't like the fair, something she couldn't even begin to understand. They were relieved they wouldn't have to pretend to be happy to take her.

After being told a hundred times to "Stay with Laura," and asked for the thousandth time if she had her jacket — which they could clearly see she did, since it was tied around her waist — Aislyn waved goodbye to her parents and trotted happily after Laura, who was already half a block away.

"Can we go on the bumper cars right away?" Aislyn asked. "I bet I'm tall enough this year. Last year I missed it by almost nothing. Of course, Mom probably wouldn't have let me go on last year even if I was tall enough and even if she had she'd be checking the time every two seconds."

Laura said nothing. Aislyn kept talking.

"And let's get dessert first! In fact, let's just get dessert. Let's get Belgian waffles with ice cream and chocolate sauce and caramel corn from the good place by the cattle barn and ..."

The sounds of the fair were getting closer. And then suddenly it was in front of them, just across the street, a miracle of light and sound and smell and whirling movement.

"... let's play that game where you drop quarters in the slot and they pile up and if you put enough in just right way you get a whole bunch back. Mom never lets me to do that because she thinks it's a waste of —"

"Don't you ever shut up?" Laura said, grabbing Aislyn's shoulders and looking her in the face. "Here's what's going to happen. I'm meeting someone."

Aislyn's smile went away.

"The Boyfriend," she said flatly. That meant she would be dragging around behind them all evening like a sack of homework they wanted to dump in a gutter. It would be worse than going to the fair with her parents, who at least pretended to want to be with her.

"Yes, and I don't want you hanging around."

Laura took twenty dollars from her pocket and shoved it in Aislyn's hand. "Take this. Mom gave it to me to buy us supper. Plus, you have your birthday money."

"What am I supposed to do?" A babyish whine crept into Aislyn's voice, and she was awfully afraid that she was going to cry.

"Go to the fair, of course!" said Laura. "See the giant slide just inside the gate? Meet me there in three hours. And I don't need to tell you that if you breathe a word of this to anyone, I'll never take you anywhere, ever again. And that would be the least of your problems with me."

Laura took two steps away, then came back again. "And don't do anything stupid. Don't leave the fairgrounds. And be at the slide on time!"

Then she spun away and jogged across the street. Aislyn spied The Boyfriend leaning against the fence and watched her sister run up to him. There was a group with The Boyfriend, all high schoolers, all slouchy and superior. Most were looking at their phones.

"Where've you been?" Aislyn heard The Boyfriend say. "I've been standing here for an hour."

She heard her sister apologize and then heard his friends laugh and say, "He's lying. We just got here."

The Boyfriend put his arm around Laura's shoulders like she was a donut and it was breakfast time. Aislyn heard her sister giggle — a strange sound, like she was copying a TV show and didn't really have it down right. They went through the gates and Aislyn lost sight of them as they blended into the crowd.

Aislyn felt shy about going into the fair by herself. She was sure everyone would know that she'd been dumped by her own sister. A large family moved past her on the sidewalk and she joined in at the tail end of them, hoping it would look like she was part of their group.

The fair gave free admission passes to all the school kids in the county. Aislyn held her pass in front of her as she approached the gate. The woman in the Lions Club jacket was chatting with the man in front of Aislyn. He was in a motorized wheelchair and had a big brown dog leashed to the chair.

The dog sniffed Aislyn's shoes.

Then it looked up at her and spoke.

"Keep an eye on your sister," the dog said.

The wheelchair started rolling. The dog went with it, leaving Aislyn with her mouth hanging open.

"I have to scan your ticket, kiddo," said the Lions Club woman. When Aislyn, still in shock, didn't move, the woman brought her scanner up to Aislyn's ticket. "The fair won't come to you, dearie. You have to go to it."

That got Aislyn moving, and two steps later she was inside the fairgrounds.

She forgot the weird moment with the talking dog. She heard thousands of voices calling and laughing, millions of machinery bits cranking and whirring, and different pop songs blasting from each ride. She smelled popcorn and fried onions, cotton candy and funnel cakes. She saw giant stuffed unicorns, an army recruiting booth and a woman with an entire band strapped to her back playing "Yellow Submarine."

All of it was almost too wonderful to exist, and she got to explore it all. By herself!

This time she would not have to stand around and wait while her parents got coffee and checked their messages. She would not have to put on a polite face when her parents met someone they knew who would keep them chatting and then interrogate her about school. She would not have to breeze through the exhibit buildings hearing them call everything "junk," even if she agreed that it was. She would not have to limit herself to rides without line-ups or to just one game of chance. When she got something to eat, she could eat it while she walked and not at a picnic table being bombarded by wet wipes every time something dripped.

Three hours. Three fabulous hours to spend as she wanted in this magical fair-land.

She spied the bumper cars. She walked over to see how many ride coupons she'd need.

A plywood bear held up a sign that read, "You must be this high to go on this ride."

Aislyn moved closer, sure that she made the grade.

"Keep an eye on your sister," the plywood bear said.

Aislyn backed away from the sign and bumped into a group of old ladies all wearing floppy purple hats.

"You almost knocked over Edith," one of them scolded.

Edith looked too sturdy for even a school bus to knock her over, but Aislyn didn't argue. She said a quick apology and hurried away, dodging through the crowd and into the nearest exhibit hall.

She walked up and down the rows of booths. There were booths that sold rock-and-roll T-shirts, booths that sold locally made beanbag toys, booths that sold handmade candles and organic dog treats, and one that sold fourteen types of salami.

Aislyn looked at everything, then stood and watched the woman at the Bricer Nicer Slicer Dicer booth turn potatoes into French fries and radishes into roses.

"Don't worry, this food won't go to waste," the woman said to the small group watching. "We feed it to the goats in the Agriculture Building at the end of the day. Buy our Nicer Slicer now for only $14.99 and I'll throw in the vegetable peeler for free. Aislyn, you need to keep an eye on your sister. Only $14.99. Fair special. Who wants one?"

Now that the chopping was done, the small crowd moved on. Aislyn hung back.

"How do you know my name?" she asked.

"Do you want to buy a Nicer Slicer? Makes a great Christmas gift."

"You said my name."

"Kid, you don't want a slicer, move on. I only get paid when I sell."

Aislyn walked on. She was feeling more than a little annoyed at all these weird reminders about her sister. Laura sure wasn't thinking about her! Why should she think about Laura?

Aislyn spent some time at the real-estate booth, looking at pictures of homes for sale and deciding which ones she'd buy if she became a millionaire. Then she moved on to what her father called Junk Food Row — what Aislyn thought of as the most heavenly-smelling place on earth!

She could have a giant cinnamon bun, warm with cream cheese frosting, or she could have a deep-fried Mars bar, or a hot dog on a stick. She could eat ice cream, cotton candy, a slice of pizza or a dozen mini donuts. It was totally up to her.

She got in line for an ice cream cone loaded with meatballs and mashed potatoes.

A woman with triplets in a stroller got in line just behind her. The triplets were wearing birthday T-shirts, lime green with drawings of birthday cake on them.

"They are one year old today," their mom said. "Longest year of my life," she added.

"They sure are cute," Aislyn said. "It's my birthday, too. I'm eleven."

"Well, happy birthday to you," one of the triplets said, in a tone that sure sounded sarcastic to Aislyn.

"You think you're such a big deal," said another.

"Having a good time, I hope," said the third. "Enjoying yourself while your sister is in trouble?"

"My sister is fine," Aislyn snapped at the babies. "She's always fine. She never thinks about me, so why should I care what's happening to her?"

"Don't shout at my babies," scolded their mom. "What's the matter with you?"

Aislyn blinked and saw that the babies were just babies again, drooling and staring at their own fingers. They were clearly not capable of making rude comments about Aislyn's relationship with her pain-in-the-neck sister.

"You're holding up the line." A man with green hair and a face full of tattoos wanted his dinner, and Aislyn was dawdling when it was her turn to order. The guy on the food truck was scowling, too.

Aislyn couldn't deal with all these adults being

mad at her. She left the line and kept walking.

She passed the most glorious food stalls, but her appetite was gone. She went into the small building under the grandstand where the giant pumpkins were. As she stood in front of the display of vegetables, they rearranged themselves to spell out SISTER in yellow squash and zucchini.

In the poultry barn, the chickens ignored her, but the geese all hissed, *"Sssssssssssister! Sssssssssssister!"* as soon as they saw her.

The animal barn was quiet when she stepped inside. She breathed in the smell of hay, watched parents point out pigs and sheep to their toddlers and watched toddlers point out cows and llamas to their parents.

Aislyn walked over to the pen full of goats. They were all asleep in the straw.

In an instant they were on their feet, up on their hind legs, forelegs on the pen fence, clamoring to get close to Aislyn, all talking at the same time.

"It's that guy she's with," one said.

"He's not a bad guy," said another.

"Deep down, he's a good guy."

"He just doesn't know it yet."

"He thinks he has to show off to his friends."

"She is not having a good time."

Goat after goat after goat spoke up, talking over each other, pushing each other out of the way so they could get their message out.

When Aislyn tried to leave, goats bit her jacket and would not let go.

"She dumped me to be with him!" Aislyn told them. "If she's not happy, that's her problem."

"Have you never made a mistake?" asked the alpaca in the next pen.

Of course she had. You couldn't be alive for eleven years and not make a mistake or two. No one could. She might make even more mistakes as more years rolled by.

"What am I supposed to do about it?" she asked the goats.

"Go to her."

"Use the Power of the Little Sister."

"You know you have it."

"But how am I supposed to find her?" The fairgrounds covered acres, and those acres were dark and full of people.

"She's on the midway," said the giant Clydesdale horse, calling out from his pen. "He's trying to get her on the Zipper."

Aislyn froze.

Then she bolted.

Laura was afraid of scary rides, and the Zipper was one of the scariest.

Aislyn ran and ran, past the farm-machinery display, through Kiddyland, through the row of games and out to the midway. She ran through crowds and dodged around ticket booths.

She arrived, breathless, at the line-up for the Zipper.

The Boyfriend and his friends were laughing at Aislyn's sister. Laura was pretending to laugh, but Aislyn saw that she was scared.

It was their turn to get on the ride. The Boyfriend put his hands on Laura's back to push her forward. Laura's legs went stiff like their dog's at vet time. The Boyfriend laughed and pushed some more. Two friends grabbed Laura's arms to pull while The Boyfriend pushed.

Aislyn threw herself into the group, right in front of Laura.

"Mom said you have to take care of me!"

"Beat it," The Boyfriend said. Aislyn ignored him.

"Mom *said*," she insisted, setting her voice to

full whine and resurrecting the pout from her long-ago past. "You have to! Or I'm telling!" She even stamped her foot.

The friends that were pulling stopped pulling and The Boyfriend stopped pushing.

"I have to go," Laura told them all. "She is such a brat. You wouldn't even believe it."

Aislyn took her sister's hand and they left the Zipper.

The county fair folded around them, the colors brighter and the smells more delicious to Aislyn than they had ever been.

Suddenly hungry, she took the twenty dollars out of her pocket and said to her sister, "Let's get supper."

Laura stopped walking.

"Thanks," she said.

Aislyn grinned. "No problem," she said.

Then Aislyn stepped with her sister into the wonder and magic of the fair.

7

Laundry

"Youngest does the laundry."

"Youngest does the laundry. Youngest does the laundry." Masud recites the annoying phrase in a high-pitched, grumpy voice. He is sick of hearing it, every single day.

"If you just did it, we wouldn't have to tell you," says Habib.

"You're not my boss."

"We are all the boss of each other. That's how we survive."

"Maybe we should ask our jailers if little Masud

can go live with the women and babies if he's not grown-up enough to do our laundry," says Sudi from across the cell.

Masud groans and gets to his feet. There are twenty-one men in his cell. Masud begins the process of going from man to man, asking if they have laundry.

"Why can't they just bring their laundry to me?" he asked Yamut one day. "Why do I have to ask?"

Yamut had been elected as the president of the cell. It was a job with extra work and no perks.

"You ask so that you have to talk to everyone," Yamut replied, "and then everyone has to talk to you. You can see if someone is not doing well. Besides, it's nice to be asked. So, ask. Be nice."

Yamut kept fifteen people alive when their raft flipped over, just with the power of his words.

Yamut was not the name he was born with. He took this name as a symbol of survival. It meant *he shall die*. Parents gave their child that name if many of their other children had already died. It was hoped that evil spirits would think the child was already cursed and leave it alone.

Before Yamut took over, there was a suicide in the cell every few days. Once there were two in one day. That's when Yamut stood up and said that from now on, they were going to be warriors in the battle against death. He put everyone on a schedule, and everyone got a job.

"You are all officers," he said. "Floor officers. Morale officers. Latrine officers. Medical officers. All of the jobs are essential. All of the jobs are of equal value and worthy of equal respect."

The floor and wall officers kept the cell clear of dust and insects. The justice officers were in charge of settling arguments. The hygiene officers made sure everyone washed every day. The morale officers planned activities and put together chess sets and other games out of things they could find in the cell and the small yard outside the cell. The religion officers organized study sessions and prayers for both the Muslims and the Christians.

Masud is the laundry officer. Being an officer does not make him like his job any better.

The mats are very close together on the floor. Masud steps carefully around each one and reluctantly asks each man if he has clothes that need washing. Most own only the clothes they are wearing. Masud politely turns his back while the brother prisoner strips and wraps up in a blanket.

"May I do your laundry?" he asks Saleem, the next youngest at seventeen. Saleem had won an early place at university, studying mathematics. Yamut made him an education officer, tasked with teaching arithmetic to Masud. It is a job he undertakes with a great sense of superiority.

Saleem hands over a shirt.

"Do you have any laundry?" he asks Tahir. Tahir is already wrapped in his sheet.

Tahir is very old — the oldest in the cell — and very learned. Back home, he was a professor of history at the university.

Tahir is in charge of record keeping. He writes down everyone's name and the names of their family members, hometowns and dates of birth. He is also in charge of the calendar. With every day so much the same, it can be hard to remember that time still rolls on.

"I am delighted to give you my clothes to wash," Tahir says, handing them over. "And I am delighted to tell you that you are no longer ten years old. Today is your birthday!"

All the men cheer, and they sing "Happy Birthday" to him.

Then, to Masud's surprise, there are presents!

Tomi, from Niger, gives him a little origami boat.

"To remind you of what brought you to this Libyan prison — and what might one day take you away."

"It's a detention center," someone says, and everyone laughs. They are in a detention center for migrants rescued from the sea, but it feels in every way like a prison.

"Except," as Saleem is fond of saying, "in a prison, you have an exit date. We might be here until the end of time."

Farad, from Afghanistan, gives Masud a picture he has drawn of a seashell.

"To remind you that the sea can also be beautiful," he says.

Yamut gives him a little statue of a tiny Masud — not as an eleven-year-old, but as a superhero, with his hands on his hips and his head held high. It even has a little cape made from a scrap of fabric.

"It's a mini-Masud," Yamut says. "I made it out of bread, a trick I learned in prison back home. You get the bread soft with a bit of water and then you mold it. I'm not good at faces, but that is you."

Masud is overwhelmed at all the presents. "You all kept it a secret from me!"

"I'm going to give you the best gift of all," Saleem says. "Just this once, I'm going to help you with the laundry."

Celebration over, Masud puts his presents on his mat and finishes collecting the clothes that need washing.

Outside their cell is a small courtyard with a high wall around it. Masud fills a bucket with water from the tap that only works some of the time. One by one he puts the articles of clothing in the bucket and swirls them around. Saleem takes the shirt or trousers and wrings it out over the bucket to preserve as much of the water as possible, then spreads the clothes out on the courtyard floor to dry.

"Are you going to try again?" Saleem asks. "If we ever get out of here?"

It is a question Masud has avoided asking himself. He got on the boat with his parents and three sisters. The boat tipped over and he floated in a dark sea until he was plucked from the water and brought to the detention center.

He knows Saleem knows this. He knows Saleem's family is still back in Jordan — miserable in a refugee camp, but alive.

He dodges the question.

"I think I'll join up with some army," he says. "Lots of armies take boys my age. I'll learn to drive a tank, and then I'll drive that tank right at the old men who destroyed my country, and I'll blow them right out of their comfortable chairs —"

Masud's last words are lost in the screech of a jet fighter overhead. He and Saleem raise their eyes to the sky.

Seconds later, the world explodes.

Dust and rocks and chunks of concrete rise in the air. Saleem and the birthday boy are thrown off their feet.

The world becomes a silent movie.

Masud sees Saleem scream without sound, raising an arm without a hand at the end. He sees men from his cell stagger out to the courtyard. He sees the hole blasted into the courtyard wall, and then he sees through it to the guards and prisoners running this way and that.

He sees the medical officers wrap a cloth around Saleem's handless arm to try to stop the bleeding.

He sees the guards come through the hole in the wall, weapons drawn, yelling silently at everyone to get back in the cell. They yell at Masud. They kick him. He tries to stand but can't. They kick him again and put the point of a rifle to his temple. The coolness of the metal actually feels good against the stabbing pain in his head.

Then Yamut is there, and others. They pick him up and carry him into the cell. He feels a wet cloth on his forehead, and his world goes kindly dark.

When he wakes up, he hears quiet moaning, quiet talking and quiet praying. Someone props him up. He drinks. He eats. The brother prisoners take care of him. He sleeps.

When he wakes up a third time, the pain in his head is less. He thinks he can stand, and he does.

"We got caught in their civil war," Yamut tells him. "Another cell block took the direct hit. They lost twelve people. We lost Saleem."

Yamut tells this to him straight on, like he is old enough to hear it.

Masud looks through the open door out to the courtyard and sees that the prison managers have wasted no time repairing the hole in the courtyard wall.

He sees that the floor officers are sweeping the floor and the wall officers are cleaning the walls. He sees that the morale officers are setting up chessboards and gathering up the scattered cards of the handmade decks. He sees that the medical officers are checking bandages. He sees that Tahir is putting the record-keeping papers in order, and that everyone not engaged in one of these tasks is in the courtyard, shaking dust from blankets and sleeping mats.

Masud sees all these men, beaten down by war, beaten down by dangerous travel, beaten down by imprisonment and beaten down by loneliness. They are all up and working. He sees men with opinions, with disagreements and with differences, all doing their part to take care of one another.

Masud decides he wants to be one of those men.

So he takes a painful step forward.

And does the laundry.

8

Free

___

Yellow is the shirt my older brother wore the last time I saw him alive.

We were walking to school together. He saw his friends in the next block and ran ahead to meet them. He ran between two gang members who were shooting at each other.

I heard the shots.

I saw him drop.

I closed my eyes and screamed.

He was ten years old. He never made it to eleven.

After the funeral, my father told my mother, "We have to leave."

"If everybody leaves," Ma said, "the gangs win."

"They killed our son," my father said. "They have already won."

"The only way they win is if we stop trying to make things better." Ma was a union organizer. She worked at a factory making cheap socks for rich feet up north.

My mother is made of iron. She won the argument. We stayed.

That was two years ago.

This morning, they killed my father.

Here is what happened.

The sock company where my mother worked moved to a country where they could pay their workers even less. Ma lost her job. She joined my father in his business, selling old clothes on the street. My sister and I helped out when we were not in school.

We were doing okay until the gangs wanted their cut.

My mother told them to go to hell. She told them their mothers were ashamed of them, that they should use their brains instead of their guns and use their lives to build up the country instead of shoving it down.

That's when they killed my father. They shot him right in the street. Right in front of us.

Then they said, "Pay us, or your little girl is next. We'll be back tomorrow for our money."

That was this morning.

I've spent the day crying and being mad and scared and throwing up and listening to everyone else crying and being mad and scared and throwing up, especially my little sister.

The house filled up with neighbors and relatives, my father's friends and Ma's union buddies. Our priest came to see us. Our teachers came to see us. Everyone hugged us. Some brought food. Some pressed money into Ma's hand.

They had quiet talks with Ma when they thought I couldn't hear.

"It's not safe for you to stay."

I've gone to the room I share with my sister and look at her curled up in a ball on her bed, sniveling.

I go over to comfort her but she says, "I want Papa, not you!" She throws Loretta, her purple bear, at me. I let her be.

The house gets quiet.

Ma comes into the room. She sits with us on

one of the beds with her strong arms holding us close. We sit like this for a long time.

Then she says one word.

"Pack."

She leaves us to it.

My sister curls back into a ball so I pack her backpack for her. I put in her favorite red dress that she'd wear all day every day if Ma would let her. I put in underwear, jeans, T-shirts and extra socks. Her purple bear is on the floor. I put that in her backpack, too. She'll want to carry it in her hands but I won't let her because she'll drop it.

I think about what else we'll need. I go out to the yard and take down the tarp that gives us shade, shake off the dirt, fold it and put it in my father's old pack along with a blanket and a length of rope to use as a clothesline. I take photographs out of frames and wrap them in plastic, along with old letters from my grandparents who have died. These can go in Ma's pack.

Now I must pack for myself.

Do I take my ribbon from debate club? My report cards? The toy horses I played with when I was small? My A+ science project on snakes of the rainforest? A little piece of twisted wood that looks like a sitting dog if you hold it the right way? The books I love?

Everything I pack, I'll have to carry. I choose some clothes, the latest report cards so I can prove I'm good in school, and that's it.

Ma finishes her own packing. We fill the empty spaces in our packs with food.

It's time to go.

I take one last look at my little house, the place where I played on the floor with my toys, where I did my homework, where we ate and laughed and argued and cried, where I hung my clothes and teased my little sister.

As I follow my mother and sister out the door, my eyes land on the calendar nailed to the kitchen wall.

Today is my birthday.

I am eleven years old.

Yellow is the baby blanket hanging out of the stroller that I have been walking behind for twenty miles.

We are part of a caravan, a long, long line of people walking to the land of the free, the place that buys the cheap socks my mother used to make.

I know that the police there sometimes shoot people the way they do in my country. I know there are gangs that steal and kill. I know there are people there who will hate me no matter how many A+ science projects I do.

I know things. I'm eleven. I'm not a baby.

But I'm hoping there will be fewer gangs and fewer police who like to shoot. And as long as my teacher is pleased with my work, it won't matter if no one else is.

Walk, walk, walk. For days, we have walked, but if I had a map of the country, it would show we have only moved an inch.

I carry my own pack on one shoulder and my father's pack on the other. My mother carries her pack and my little sister's pack, and sometimes she carries my little sister, too.

We walk alongside busy highways and down quiet streets. We follow the stroller with the yellow baby blanket and just keep walking.

Yellow are the flames in the little campfires that dot the darkness and keep us company in the night.

My mother has organized an area for women

and children who are traveling on their own.

"We all know someone who's been attacked on this journey north," she says. "We all know of people who have disappeared along the way. We will not let that happen on this trip! We will look out for each other!"

I offer to help stand watch. Ma kisses my cheek — in front of everyone! — and says my father would be proud of me.

Ma settles my sister, who clutches the purple Loretta, into the blanket under the tarp we've draped over a tree branch and snuggles in with her. I join a few women sitting around a nearby campfire.

Soon I hear Ma's snoring. It makes us laugh because it's so loud, and it makes me feel good because I've heard it all my life. It's a lullaby.

I listen to the women talk quietly about the people they've left behind and the people they're hoping to see again in the land of the free. Some have husbands who went ahead of them. Some have sisters. Some, like me, have nobody and are running away to save their lives. They treat me like one of them, and I feel proud and grown-up.

We talk and keep watch over the meadow of

tarps and blankets full of sleeping people, until someone taps me on the shoulder and sends me off to bed.

Yellow is the egg sitting on the rice beside the tortilla on the paper plate the smiling stranger holds out to me.

"How much does it cost?" I ask, my stomach rumbling.

"No charge, my friend. It's free. A present. Go ahead. There's enough for your family, too. Go on, eat."

We started walking this morning while the sun was still sleeping. We walked while it rose. We walked while it climbed in the sky.

Now that the sun is going to bed, we have finally stopped walking for the day. We are sitting on the steps of a church, looking out at the town square full of travelers and townspeople who are feeding the travelers. I am so tired I can barely breathe.

"Eat," the smiling stranger says again. "You are our guests. One day I might be in your shoes."

We eat the food and we drink the water someone else gives us. My mother perks up and she starts barking orders. I string the rope to hang laundry. A woman from the town shoos me away.

"I'll help your mother," she says. "You go play."

I look at Ma. She nods and smiles, and I almost slip away on my own but of course she says, "Take your sister."

There are people bathing in the river. We take off our outer clothes and wade in. The water washes off the dust and sweat of the day.

I can't tell which way the river is flowing. Maybe it is flowing south and will carry our dust back to our home. Maybe it is flowing north and our dust will reach the land of the free before we do.

My sister slips in the mud. A stranger helps her up, then moves away before we can say thank you. I help an old man up the riverbank. Then I move away before he can thank me.

Yellow is the lightning that is chasing the train.

We are on top of a train called The Beast, all of us caravaners together on the roof of every car. We are doing things my mother would never allow us to do in ordinary life.

The train is moving fast.

The lightning is moving faster.

The rain reaches us. I take the tarp out of my

father's pack and cover everyone who can fit under it.

It is dark under the tarp. When the lightning flashes, all I see is yellow.

Yellow is the badge on the border guard's chest. His blank face tells me he is not interested in our story. He barely looks at us.

"We are here for asylum," my mother tells him.

"You are here illegally," he replies.

It takes three of them to handcuff her. It takes two more to hold back my sister who fights to get to our mother.

I try to run from one to the other, to pull them away from the guards, but I am hauled away and loaded onto a bus full of children. The guard pushes me into a scat. I'm shaking and feeling like I'm going to throw up. All around me kids are crying — little kids, big kids and in-between kids like me.

I see the guards carry my little sister onto the bus. They sit her up front with the other young ones. I try to get to her but the guard tells me to get back in my seat.

The bus starts moving. I don't know where our

backpacks are. I don't know where my sister's bear is.

I don't know where our mother is.

Yellow is the line down the middle of the hallway.

"Walk against the wall! You! Back in line! Didn't you hear me? Against the wall!"

The guard yells in English. The kids who know English translate for those who don't. When the guard's back is turned, I dart out of line just long enough to spot my sister. An older girl has her hand on my sister's shoulder.

We are taking care of each other in this new world just as we did in the old one.

Yellow is the ceiling light that shines all day and all night.

The light shows through my eyelids even when my eyes are closed.

I am in a cage full of children in a room full of cages. We have rubber mats to sleep on and foil blankets that are not soft and not comforting. There is crying.

We are tired and hungry and sick and filthy and fed up and scared.

We can't go to the bathroom unless the guards

let us out of the cages and take us. I don't want to have to beg to be able to use a toilet.

There are no windows in this big, big room, and no clocks. It is day when the guards say it's day. It is night when the guards say it's night.

We look at them through the bars and they look back at us, and I wonder if this will now be my life forever and forever.

Yellow is the plastic chair that I am sitting on in the playroom. My sister sits in a chair beside me, coloring a picture of a clown. The chair is too small for me.

We are out of the cages and in a different detention center. There are no bars, but we can't leave. There are books and toys in the playroom, but we don't know where our mother is. It's been days since we have seen her. Days and days.

One leg of my chair is shorter than the other legs. I rock the chair back and forth. At first I don't even notice I'm doing it. The woman in charge speaks Spanish and she tells me to stop. I want to ask what difference it makes to her whether I rock on the chair or not. I decide not to ask.

Then I do it.

"What difference does it make to you how I sit?"

She looks surprised that I've spoken, but she has an answer.

"It's government property."

"It was like this before I sat in it," I point out.

She tells me to watch my bad attitude.

When the woman's back is turned, I rock again. Just a little.

There's a small window in the playroom, high up on the wall. We're not supposed to stand on the furniture — it says so in the list of rules posted by the door — but I don't care. I pull over a table and get on top of it. By standing on my tiptoes, I can see outside.

I see a high fence topped with coils of razor wire. There is a street on the other side of the fence, a normal street with cars and cyclists and a woman walking her dog. The dog pees on the fence.

I see a gas station and a 7-Eleven and a shop that sells car parts. I watch someone go into the 7-Eleven and I watch someone else come out of it, sipping a very large drink through a straw. I think about what I would like to buy at that 7-Eleven, if I could just leave this jail, if I just had money. I'd get a large orange soda and a giant bag of popcorn.

Several vans pull into the 7-Eleven parking lot. People get out. They are holding signs and megaphones. The signs read, "Free the Children/Libera a los ninos." They cross the street and stand right against the fence. They put the megaphones to their faces and they start to sing to all of us inside the jail. The words are a jumble but I can hear the melodies.

It sounds terrible.

It sounds wonderful.

They sing and sing and when the police come and try to stop them, they just keep on singing.

Kids in the playroom notice what I'm doing and they join me on the table. I get down to give them more room.

I sing a song my mother and father used to sing to me.

The list of rules says nothing about that.

Yellow is the door we stare at us as we wait for something to happen.

They say our mother is coming to get us. They

say they will take her to us as soon as they clear up some paperwork. Then she will walk through that door.

My little sister is kicking the leg of my chair. Even though she is annoying, I let her kick. I don't want Ma to come through the yellow door and find us arguing. My sister holds another bear. This one is green. She picked it up in the playroom and refused to put it down. The guards asked me to help them get it from her. I pretended I didn't hear them.

Just when it feels like I will lose all patience with bears and sisters and kicking and waiting, the yellow door opens and our mother is there. We are in her arms, crying and hugging, and it really is her, solid and sure and strong and mine.

The guard leads us to the exit.

I know I should say thank you. That would be good manners.

I decide not to. Then I do it.

"Thank you," I say.

"You're welcome," says the guard. "And good luck."

We walk outside, the three of us holding on to each other. We get to the high fence and wait for the guard to open the gate.

I look back at the jail. In case any kids are standing on the tabletop, looking out the window, I smile and wave.

Then we step through the gate.

And into the land of the free.

9

Nails

The Two Junes and Marmalay were going to get their nails done.

The Two Junes were called that because their birthdays were both in June. Their real names were Bettina and Lally. Both had long bouncy hair. Marmalay saw a lot of that hair because when they were all out together, the Two Junes filled the sidewalk and Marmalay walked behind.

Marmalay's hair was short, cut in the latest pixie style. Her hair used to be long, but when she was six, the Junes put bubblegum in it. Mum had to cut the gum out, and she kept taking her for hair-cuts ever since.

The Junes hadn't called her Bubblehead in years, but Marmalay was sure they were still thinking it.

The three mums walked behind the three girls. The mums had been best friends since school and were all pregnant with the girls at the same time.

Marmalay was born first, in April. Being the oldest should have given her an advantage, but it didn't. The trio was run by Lally, who used to have such vicious tantrums when she didn't get her way that the other two just got in the habit of giving in. Second in command was Bettina because, well, they were the Two Junes.

The three girls had spent all their birthdays together since they were babies.

"When we are a hundred years old and living in the home," the mums joked, "you will all come to us so we can still celebrate together."

Their mums had ten years of pictures of them sitting with cakes. Today would mark the start of the eleventh set of birthday pictures. After getting their nails done, they were going to the tea shop on the North Pier for cake.

Marmalay had wanted to go to Party On Nails,

the new salon with the TV ads near the Central Pier, but it was already booked by the time her mum called them. Nail parties were all the rage in Blackpool. Mum had to call several salons before she found one that could take all three girls at the same time.

The Fancy Bright Vietnamese Nail Bar was tucked away behind the Marks and Spencer. The window held three bamboo plants in a blue flowerpot, a smiling Buddha and a poster of all the nail colors and designs on offer.

Marmalay and the Two Junes oohed and aahed at the choices and pointedly ignored any suggestions made by their mothers.

"I like the moons," said Lally.

Marmalay liked the moons herself, but she couldn't choose them now because Lally already did. Really, it was *her* birthday. She should be able to pick first.

"Here's one that looks like art deco," said Bettina, who'd heard the phrase on a home decorating show and wouldn't stop using it.

The Junes made their choices — crescent moons on indigo for Lally, gold crowns on sparkly silver for Bettina — then went inside the salon with their mums. Marmalay stared at the poster, hoping something great would leap out at her.

And it did!

"I'm getting the eyes!" she announced. "On Sunflower Yellow."

It was an outrageous choice, much bolder than moons or crowns.

"You want eyes painted on your fingernails?" Mum asked. Then she laughed. "Why not? You only turn eleven once."

They went into the salon.

Mum spoke to the manager, a middle-aged woman sitting behind a desk. The manager smiled and invited Marmalay to take a seat at a nail station. The Two Junes were already getting their cuticles cleaned. There was no attendant at Marmalay's station, and no other customers.

Marmalay sat there by herself for a few moments, not sure what to do. She looked over at her mum but the mums had made themselves at home on the plastic chairs in the waiting area, chatting away as they thumbed through the selection of newspapers and magazines on the low, round table.

Moments ticked on. The manager was at her

desk, her back to Marmalay. The Two Junes were doing the whisper-giggle. Marmalay avoided looking at them, sure they were making fun of her.

Finally she spoke up.

"Excuse me," she said to the manager. "Is there another manicurist?"

The manager turned around, looked with surprise at the empty chair at Marmalay's station, then opened a side door beside a supply shelf. She hollered up the stairs in a language Marmalay assumed was Vietnamese.

Soon the third attendant appeared.

The young woman wiped her eyes as she put her arms through her pink smock and sat down at the station.

"And smile!" hissed the manager in English before going back to her desk.

The attendant kept her eyes lowered as she reached for Marmalay's hands to begin the manicure. She did not smile.

Marmalay hated being told to smile herself, so she was all sympathy for the attendant. Still, no smile made her think that the manicurist didn't really *want* to do her nails. It was an uncomfortable feeling.

"It's quiet in here," Lally said. "At Party On Nails they had Taylor Swift."

"When were you at Party On Nails?" Marmalay asked before her brain could stop her.

"Oh, weren't you with us?" asked Lally.

"Remember the cupcakes we had there?" Bettina exclaimed. "Will we be having cupcakes here?" she asked, even though there was clearly not a cupcake in sight.

"Cupcakes are so yesterday," Marmalay replied.

It *was* quiet in the salon, even with the mums chattering and the Two Junes being all Juney. None of the manicurists were talking. Their eyes were down and their mouths were shut.

It reminded Marmalay of walking into a room with her parents' arguing hovering in the air, even though they'd gone quiet as soon as they heard her footsteps.

"It's my birthday," she said to her attendant, to start a conversation and brighten the mood. "I'm eleven."

The manicurist didn't even look at her.

"Mani," Marmalay read off the nametag on the manicurist's smock. "That's a pretty name. I was named May after my great-grandmother, but that's too plain. I love grapefruit marmalade, so I put the two together and called myself Marmalay."

Nothing. No response.

Some fun birthday this was turning out to be.

She gave up on the attendant and listened to the mums admiring the latest fashions worn by the royals.

"Their handbags always match their outfits," Bettina's mum said, fluttering a magazine. "How many handbags do they have, do you think?"

"They must have whole closets just for purses."

"Maybe they share," suggested Marmalay's mum. "One royal closet full of Gucci and ..."

Marmalay could tell her mum was searching for the name of another swanky handbag maker and was coming up empty.

"Of course they don't share," Lally's mum said. "Share?" Lally's mum spoke the last word as if Marmalay's mum had suggested the royals shared knickers.

"They certainly do work hard," Marmalay's mum said quickly. "Oh, here's a piece on the opening day of the Ascot."

Marmalay was surprised. Her mum had no use for the royal family. She liked the queen, of course, as a person, but thought the rest of them should get proper jobs and earn their own way, just like the rest of Britain. She was always going on about it.

But not today. Today her mum was gushing over a silly hat and remarking on the posture of some old duke on a horse.

Marmalay tried to tune out the mums but there was nothing else to focus on except the sniggering of the Two Junes.

She was trapped in this boring nail bar with a manicurist who clearly did not want to be painting her nails, celebrating her birthday with people who — apart from her mum — she didn't even like.

I don't like the Two Junes, she thought, seeing that fact clearly in her mind for the very first time. I don't like either of them.

She rolled that thought around in her head, wondering what it might mean.

"I see that driver decided to plead guilty," Marmalay's mum said, rattling a newspaper.

"What driver?"

"That lorry driver. The one who killed all those people."

"What people?" Marmalay asked, eager for the distraction. "Did he run them over?"

"No, no. You remember, luv. I'm sure we talked about it when it happened. Thirty-nine Vietnamese migrants suffocated to death in the back of his lorry. Oh, it says here that ten of them were just teenagers. I didn't know that. Poor lambs."

"What do you mean, poor lambs?" Lally's mum asked.

"Well, it must be a terrible way to die," Mum said. "In the dark, grasping for a breath. And so young."

"No one asked them to come here," said Bettina's mum.

"No, but look, the sister of one of the dead girls said she was coming here to work in a nail salon."

"Taking our jobs," said Lally's mum.

"But two of the boys were only fifteen," Marmalay's mum said. "Only four years older than Marmy."

Marmalay bit her lip to keep from screaming out, "Don't call me Marmy! I've told you and told you!"

"Marmy," sniggered Lally. "Barmy Marmy."

The new version of Bubblehead.

Marmalay had had enough. It was her birthday!

"Sod off!" she yelled at Lally and Bettina. "You both think you're clever but you're not. You're just … average!"

"Oh, look," said Marmalay's mum in a voice a bit too loud and a bit too bright. "The queen's chef is sharing his secret recipes that he feeds the corgis!"

"She takes such good care of those dogs," said Bettina's mum.

The mums prattled. The Two Junes glared at Marmalay and mouthed obscenities at her. Marmalay turned away from them. She looked at Mani and her two colleagues. Their eyes were still lowered as they concentrated on their work.

The long birthday stretched before her, and the Two Junes' birthdays after that. She didn't think she could stand it.

"We're done," said Lally. She and Bettina left their nail stations with their hands spread out before them. "Do we have to wait for Marmy?"

"May *is* in a bit of a mood," Lally's mum said to Marmalay's mum. "Perhaps we should go on to the tea shop. Give you a moment to put a party face on her."

"Yes, why don't you?" said Mum. "Marmalay and I will catch you up. Oh, and I'll get the girls' nails. My treat."

"Right, then," said Bettina's mum.

"Barmy Marmy," Bettina and Lally chanted as they left the salon.

It got quiet again in the salon. Mani finished Marmalay's nails.

Marmalay stared at her hands. Ten new eyes stared back at her.

The better to see with, she thought.

"Thank you," she said to Mani.

It seemed like there was something more that should be said, but Marmalay had no idea what that was. In front of her, Mani was tidying the work station. Behind her, Mum was paying for the manicures. Marmalay stood by the nail station, trying to figure out what it was that needed to be said.

And then she knew.

"I'm glad you're here," she said to Mani.

Mani looked up at her and almost smiled.

"Happy birthday," she said to Marmalay.

Out on the street with Mum, Marmalay felt a rush of happiness.

"Let's not meet them at the tea shop," she said to her mother. "Let's just … not."

Mum looked at her daughter and slowly nodded as a smile spread across her face.

Then, even though Marmalay was eleven, she took her mother's hand, and they stepped away together down the street.

10

Supper

Len set the last basket of bread on the last table and stood back to see if anything was missing.

Cutlery? Check. Napkins? Wrapped around the cutlery, so, check. Margarine? Check.

Salt and pepper!

He headed for the kitchen. Another volunteer — Joline, the choir leader — was already rolling the cart full of salt and pepper shakers into the church hall.

"Two sets on each," Joline said, as if he didn't know, as if he hadn't been here the last Monday of

every month since he was nine. But Joline had to
be bossy. The choir could be an unruly bunch.

Len and Joline zoomed the serving cart around
the hall, putting two salt and pepper shakers on
each table. Another volunteer followed with pickle
trays.

They were ready.

"Let them in!"

Len put on gloves and a ridiculous-looking hairnet that he would have hated except that everyone
else was wearing one, too, and looked just as ridic-
ulous. He stood behind the serving table between
Dorothy, who taught him in Sunday school when
he was little, and Mr. Zimmer, who always sat at
a pew near the front with his wife. Len had been
looking at the back of Mr. Zimmer's head of gray
hair every Sunday for his entire life.

Len's dad came out of the kitchen carrying a
large metal steamer tray full of hot stew, followed
by his mom and more volunteers with more food.
A plastic basin full of coleslaw was placed in front
of Len.

"One scoop each to start," he was told. Again,
as if he had never done this before.

Len draped a dish towel over half of the salad

bin. Half of each serving dish had to be covered
for health reasons. He adjusted his gloves which
were a bit too big for his hands and looked out at
the hall filling up with hungry people.

He saw many familiar faces. The old man with
the long beard and no teeth who always wore a
tie. The woman with three little kids, whose oldest kid always helped the youngest. The tall man
who always sat at the back of the hall, ate fast and
left quickly. The mom and daughter, both ancient,
both tiny and stooped over, who delivered flyers
door to door in all weather and brought plastic
containers to carry home half their meal.

"Beef and tomato stew tonight," Mr. Zimmer
said, lifting the lid off his tray. "Rice, too. Good
and filling on a night like this."

Steam rose from the dishes. The November
evening was being very November — cold, wet,
gloomy, a long time to Christmas and an eternity
to spring.

"I like stew," Len said, but he doubted there
would be enough left over for the volunteers.

The guests ate more on cold nights. Maybe the
cold made them hungrier. Maybe they were taking
their time so they didn't have to go back out into it.

It didn't matter. There was always food at home. On volunteer nights, he and his parents usually had grilled cheese sandwiches when they got back.

People continued to file in. Some came in a group, greeted friends and sat together. Some came in alone and did their best to sit alone. They took off their wet jackets and draped them over the backs of their chairs. There were hangers by the door, but no one used them. They were afraid their things would get stolen. Some kept their coats on while they ate.

An older woman with a cane walked slowly into the hall, followed by someone wearing a hoodie. As the old woman was helped off with her coat, Len caught a glimpse of the hooded face.

Len felt his body stiffen.

It was Cee.

Cee had tormented Len from second grade on. When Len wore a red shirt, Cee called him a tulip, and then he was Tulip Boy for months. If Len answered in class, Cee was right there, repeating the answer in a high squeaky voice. "A hundred and forty-four." "The War of 1812." "Victoria is the capital of British Columbia." And everyone would laugh.

Even when Cee didn't do that, Len was afraid he would, and he stopped raising his hand.

He was tripped on the playground. Books on his desk were swept to the floor. A bottle of glue was emptied into his boots.

Always, there were threats. "Look my way again, I'll poke your eyes out." "You'd better run all the way home today!"

Sandwiches smashed. Homework stolen and ripped apart. Paintings he did in art class that the teacher hung on the wall got curse words scrawled on them.

It always happened away from the teachers and was never bad enough that Len told his parents. He doubted they could do anything about it anyway.

And now Cee was here. And Len was wearing a hairnet.

It was bad. It was very, very bad.

Len wanted to leave the serving line and hide in the kitchen, but they were saying grace. The amen still hovered in the air as guests pushed back their chairs and lined up for supper.

Please let him go to the other line. Please let him go to the other line, Len prayed.

The serving table was set up with two trays of everything, arranged so that there could be two separate serving lines. People got their meals faster that way. If Cee went to the other serving line, maybe he wouldn't see Len.

Maybe he wouldn't look up. Lots of people didn't, even though all the servers said hello and "Would you like …" whatever it was they were serving. They got their food with their heads down, ate it with their heads down and left the hall without once looking up.

Others were chatterers. They knew Len, always asked him about school and said, "Thanks, very much."

On the outside, Len acted normal, smiling and spooning out salad. Inside, his heart was beating strong as he tried to keep track of where Cee was.

And then Cee was in front of him.

"Deer in the headlights" was one of Len's father's corny expressions, but Len never understood it until this moment.

Cee stood with his plate extended. Already full of rice and stew and vegetables, there was just enough room on it for a scoop of salad.

Len had the salad ready to go. He saw Cee staring at him.

"They make us wear these hairnets," Len said. "The health department makes us. If we don't wear them, the police will come and shut us down. Probably the whole SWAT team would smash in through the windows ..."

Len's voice trailed off.

The church hall doubled as a gym. It had no windows.

Len shook his head. There was no point. He plopped the coleslaw down on Cee's plate.

"What do you say, Cecil?" asked the old woman with the cane who had come up to the serving table with him.

"Thank you," Cee mumbled, glaring at Len.

Len served the old woman, and she and Cee went back to their seats.

Len felt like crying. His hairnet would be all over the school tomorrow. Hell, it would be all over social media before he got home. Cee had probably already taken his picture. He'd be called Hairnet Boy or Granny Lenny.

He had to stay put and be polite to Dorothy and to Mr. Zimmer while guests returned to the serving table for seconds. Len was relieved to see Cee go to the other line.

As he'd predicted, all the food got eaten. Len helped clear the serving table and was about to take the trolley out to collect the dirty dishes (starting in the corner farthest from Cee) when Joline clapped her hands to get everyone's attention.

"We invite everyone to stay in their seats for a very special dessert."

The lights in the hall dimmed a bit, and Len heard singing.

"Happy birthday to you!"

Len's mother and father carried in an enormous slab of a cake with eleven candles on it. The guests in the hall joined in the singing, and there was a lot of clapping when he blew out his candles.

Len helped serve out the cake, hoping Cee wouldn't come up, hoping Cee hated cake, that he was allergic to flour and that if he so much as got near cake his eyeballs would explode.

The old woman came up to the table. Cee wasn't with her.

"Could I have two pieces?" she asked. "My grandson is in a mood."

Len knew that the old woman could not manage

two pieces of cake and walk with her cane. He could pretend not to know this, but then he would just feel like a jerk.

He carried the cake for the old lady and waited until she settled herself in the chair before he put the dessert down in front of her.

He put the other piece down in front of Cee.

Then he just stood.

I'm eleven now, he thought. Something has to change.

"What are you staring at, Hairnet?" Cee growled, pushing the plate of cake away. "I suppose you'll blab about this all over school."

Blab about what?

Then all of a sudden, Len knew.

Cee was ashamed to be at the free supper.

Cee was ashamed to be hungry.

"I won't blab," said Len, "if you won't blab about the hairnet."

Cee searched Len's face. Len saw something soften in Cee's scowl.

"Deal," said Cee, looking down.

Len started to walk away, then stopped. "All the chairs have to be stacked when we're done. Stacks of ten."

"So?" said Cee.

"We could use some help."

"I'll think about it," Cee said. He ate a bite of birthday cake.

Len cleared tables and took a trolley full of dirty dishes to the kitchen. When he came out, Cee was stacking chairs.

Len stepped toward his enemy.

There were a lot of chairs to stack.

ALSO BY DEBORAH ELLIS

Nine poignant and empowering
short stories from the author of
The Breadwinner.

———————

The seated child. With a single powerful image,
Deborah Ellis draws our attention to nine children
and the situations they find themselves in, often
through no fault of their own. In each story, a
child makes a decision and takes action, be that a
tiny gesture or a life-altering choice.

Jafar is a child laborer in a chair factory and
longs to go to school. Sue sits on a swing as she

and her brother wait to have a supervised visit with their father at the children's aid society. Gretchen considers the lives of concentration camp victims during a school tour of Auschwitz. Mike survives seventy-two days of solitary as a young offender. Barry squirms on a food court chair as his parents tell him that they are separating. Macie sits on a too-small time-out chair while her mother receives visitors for tea. Noosala crouches in a fetid, crowded apartment in Uzbekistan, waiting for an unscrupulous refugee smuggler to decide her fate.

These children find the courage to face their situations in ways large and small, in this eloquent collection from a master storyteller.

☆ "Beautifully wrought, the collection will appeal to thoughtful readers who appreciate Ellis' other globally-aware works … An excellent choice for all collections." — *Booklist*, starred review

"Ellis's protagonists share the common goal of survival — be it emotional, physical, or both — and her thought-provoking collection should spark wide-ranging discussions about choice and injustice." — *Publishers Weekly*